SOCIOPATH

a thriller

VICTOR METHOS

Copyright 2013 Victor Methos
Kindle/Print Edition
License Statement

This ebook is licensed for your personal enjoyment only. This ebook may not be re-sold or given away to other people. If you would like to share this book with another person, please purchase an additional copy for each recipient. If you're reading this book and did not purchase it, or it was not purchased for your use only, then please return and purchase your own copy. Thank you for respecting the hard work of this author. Please note that this is a work of fiction and any similarity to persons, living or dead, is purely coincidental.

Prologue

Screams filled the forest as the darkness closed in.

Her legs were cut and bleeding from the bushes that tugged at her exposed flesh as she sprinted in the night. It was difficult to see and the trees were so tall they occasionally blocked out the moon, the only light she had.

She was sobbing and felt tears rolling down her cheeks as she came to a small stream. Careful not to fall on the slick rocks, she spread her arms for balance and waded across. On the other side she looked back and saw the dark figure come out of the brush, the hunting knife gleaming in his hand. He stood silent as a shadow and she felt his eyes on her body.

She dashed up the embankment. Digging her fingers into the soft forest floor, she rose over the top and tried to run down too quickly. She felt her knee give out and she hit the ground hard and rolled until she hit a tree, pain shooting through her ribs. She was on her back only a moment before lifting herself up.

The forest was cold at night and filled with noise. Owls and coyotes and crows. She could hear them all on the periphery of her consciousness, like the voices one ignores at a restaurant when focusing on their own conversation.

Trying again to run, she collapsed onto her stomach and grunted in pain. Her knee had been injured snowboarding years ago, and she'd had surgery to repair it, but it had never been the same. Now it was tattered and she felt the instability as she pushed herself off the ground.

Hobbling through the dense forest, the smell of wet pine in her nostrils, she heard footsteps behind her.

"No! Please! Please don't."

The figure grabbed her as she tried to run and it threw her to the ground. She pulled herself up using a tree for balance and felt a burning sensation across her stomach. She looked down to see her organs slipping out of the slit in her belly. She tried to run again, but it was too late.

A blow to her head and she was on the ground. The figure spun her onto her back, the knife gleaming in the moonlight.

JON STANTON

I exploded out of the ocean and sucked in breath like a drowning man. The surfboard was connected to my ankle and I felt it tugging at me from somewhere behind.

The Pacific was warm and I wondered if I really needed the wetsuit. I treaded water for a few minutes before reaching down and pulling on the cord. As the surfboard came near, I climbed on top.

I could see Emma on the beach. Sitting on a towel with an umbrella over her, reading a magazine. Her body was tan and slender as opposed to the pasty white she'd been when we'd first arrived in Honolulu almost eight months ago. It was a vacation, but we'd both had an eye toward moving here, and after the first week we knew it was for us.

I paddled in until I caught my wave. The wave was slow but I stood and eased into shore. She looked at me and smiled and it sent butterflies up and down my stomach. She had that effect on me. Not only was Emma a brilliant chemist with a mind far superior to my own, she was strikingly beautiful in that appealing, librarian kind of way that young boys daydream about. Men were always hitting on her wherever we went and she thought that it offended me, and it never did. But I didn't find it flattering either that other men saw me as so minor a threat that they could hit on my fiancé in front of me.

I wasn't muscular or brutish looking. Physicality had never been one of my strong suits. In fact if it wasn't for surfing and jogging I wouldn't get any physical activity at all.

My own skin was dark brown and my hair had developed blond highlights again and appeared washed out. I slicked my hair back and away from my eyes as I saw Emma pick up my cell phone and answer.

When I hit the shallows I unhooked my board and lifted it as I came ashore. Emma had hung up the phone, and waited until I lay next to her before placing her hand over my chest and running her fingers across it.

"I think I like you in a wet suit," she said. "You look like an adorable little seal."

"Let's hope the sharks don't feel the same way. Who was on the phone?"

"Someone named Kyle Vidal. He asked that you call him when you get a sec."

"Vidal? You sure that was his name?"

"Yeah. Why?"

"I only know one Kyle Vidal but I haven't spoken to him in about a decade."

"Who is he?"

I hesitated. This was the hardest part of any day. The time when, invariably, my past life came back and showed me who I had been.

I retired from the San Diego Police Department as a homicide detective years ago. After that, I tried the life of a private investigator, and though the money was great, as Emma had pointed out to me, it wasn't that much different from being a cop. When we moved to Honolulu I abandoned it and starting teaching full-time at the University of Hawaii in their psychology and criminal justice departments.

Teaching had always been relaxing for me. Something about passing down knowledge to future generations appealed to me, but I had very ... specific knowledge, and I didn't know how many people could understand it. Or that the students would want to if they could.

Emma had taken a job at a private laboratory that paid four times what I made as a professor. She was one of the leading physical chemists in the country and probably could have had a tenured position in any university she wanted. But she stayed here, with me, because she saw how good the sunshine and sea was for me.

I realized I'd hesitated too long and she knew something was wrong.

"What is it, Jon?"

"He's with the Behavioral Science Unit at the FBI. I'm sure he's just calling wanting advice on a case."

"We came out here to get away from that."

"I know. I'm not calling him back."

She smiled and kissed me and then went back to her magazine.

2

We left the beach later that afternoon and stopped at a sandwich shack we both loved. We'd discovered it by accident. Our power had gone out during a particularly brutal rainstorm and we couldn't cook so we went out and explored the streets. We had to cover our heads with a newspaper because we hadn't researched Hawaii enough to know that we would need umbrellas. Emma had held my hand as we went up the street and nearly went into an expensive Italian restaurant. She'd then looked back and saw this gray shack with red lettering announcing the best pulled pork sandwich in the islands.

The sun was shining down on my head and warming me now, and just thinking back to the rain put me in a different mood. Weather affected people in strange ways, and I always thought it would be an interesting research project to plot cultural idiosyncrasies with the climate the people lived in.

We sat in a booth by the window and she ordered a Cherry Coke, orange juice and two pulled pork sandwiches with fries. She was twirling the straw in the glass and not looking me in the eyes.

It had been the call. The last time I received a call like that I had to kill someone who nearly killed me, down in a dark hole underneath Joshua Tree. A young girl crawling through a tunnel to safety as I stayed with the monster who had taken her.

The stink of the hole didn't leave me for several weeks and I remembered constant showers and laundry. Emma told me she couldn't smell anything, but I knew it was there, and I'd smell it in the night and it would wake me up.

Eventually, I had to burn the clothes I had been wearing that day.

"I'm not calling him back."

"I know," she said.

"Then why the long face?"

"I just don't like being reminded of it."

"It was who I was, not who I am. Not anymore."

"You can't change who you are, Jon. You loved what you did. I see you sometimes late at night on the laptop when you think I'm asleep. You're reading news stories about cases in your old district."

I had nothing to say, so I kept quiet.

"Do you miss it?"

"No."

"Be honest with me," she said.

"No, I don't miss it. I'm curious."

"Why?"

The sandwiches came and I laid the napkin on my lap and took a bite, hoping she would forget to follow up. Though I doubt she forgot, she didn't ask about it again and we ate in silence. It was the first time since coming to Honolulu we couldn't think of anything to say to each other.

"I think you should get a new cell phone," she said.

"What would that do? He's a supervisor at the FBI. If he wanted to find me he could."

She exhaled. "Why can't they leave you alone?"

I shook my head. "I don't know."

3

Our beach house sat on a quarter acre in Hawaii Kai, one of the most exclusive sections of Honolulu made up of homes on a stretch of beach and the surrounding hills. I went out to the patio and sat in a chair, sipping ice water and watching the waves roll in and break on the sand. The wind was blowing and my hair would fall in front of my sunglasses and then be lifted again.

Emma had gone to her yoga class and wouldn't be back for a while. I took out my phone and dialed my ex-wife's number. She lived somewhere in Boston. Her new husband had been a halfback with the Chargers before being traded to the Patriots. Last I'd heard from my son, he'd blown out both his knees and had to leave the NFL. They were now living in a quiet suburb while he started a real estate business.

I let Melissa move with the boys wherever she wanted. My oldest, Mathew, told me once that she needed him more than I needed him. I understood the need for a son to look after his mother and I never protested, even though I could have forced the issue and gotten them to stay in San Diego with me. Considering that I'd moved now too, it was a good call.

No one answered and I tried Matt's cell.

"Hey Dad."

"How are ya, buddy?"

"Good."

"What're you up to?"

"I'm over at my friend Andy's house. Just playing Xbox."

"Your mom told me you got straight A's this term. That true?"

"Kind of. I got two A minuses."

"In what?"

"Japanese and pottery."

"I think those can be forgiven. I'm sending you over a present."

"What is it?"

"You'll have to wait and see."

"Just tell me, Dad."

I grinned. "Sorry, buddy. Anticipation makes it that much sweeter." I sipped my water. "Where's Johnny?"

"He's right here. Hold on."

I heard the phone transfer hands.

"Hi Dad."

"Hey, kiddo. You hanging out with your brother today?"

"Yeah."

Though he was now ten, I still remembered him as the tubby one-year-old running around in his diaper, his fingers stained with food and his lips surrounded by a dim tint of juice.

"Are you taking care of your mom?"

"Dad … can I come live with you?"

My heart dropped. I didn't say anything for a moment. "Why would you want to live with me, Johnny? Your mom and brother are in Boston."

"I miss you. I wanna come live there."

I swallowed and looked out over the ocean. I had been alone until I'd met Emma and I'd gotten used to that loneliness. As much as I loved them, the thought of them living with me filled me with a gray dread, fearing that I would be exposing them to things they shouldn't be exposed to, that they would remind me every day of what I could lose at just the squeezing of a trigger by madness. Every second I would be living at the edge of a cliff, thinking of the things the world could do to them and knowing I would be unable to stop it.

"Let me talk to your mom first."

"If she says yes can I come?"

"Let me talk to her and then we'll talk again."

"Okay. Love you, Dad."

"Love you too."

I hung up and placed the phone down on my lap. I stared at the ocean about as long as I had spoken on the phone and counted six waves. Some type of bird, probably a heron, dipped under the water and I watched for him to come out when the phone rang. I looked down; it was a Facetime call.

I opened Facetime and answered and Kyle Vidal's tan face came on the screen. I knew Kyle from only a few encounters at law enforcement training seminars. He'd offered me a position once with the Bureau and I'd turned it down. I told him I wanted less red tape, not more, and he never brought it up again.

"Jon. How are you?"

"I'm fine."

"You get my message earlier?"

"I did."

"But you weren't going to call me back, were you?"

"Maybe you didn't hear, but I retired a couple of years ago."

"No, I heard. David told me. That's actually why I'm calling. Sorry about the Facetime but I just thought you would be more likely to answer if you could see me."

Why would you think that?

"What can I do for you, Kyle? If it's about David's message, I didn't call him back either."

"David's actually the reason I'm calling ... I don't exactly know how to say this. I know you two were pretty close. He's passed away, Jon."

I went silent.

David and I had met on a case nearly fifteen years ago, my first year as a uniformed patrol officer. It was a DUI that turned into a big child pornography bust and the Bureau had come in for assistance. He showed me the ropes, what to say to my superiors and how to spin the events on a police report. We'd stayed friends after that and went on three vacations together with our families, until his wife passed away a number of years ago.

I still remember his smile the time we caught a trout the size of a baseball bat in Lake Tahoe. I saw his face when his wife passed, hardened, like it had been carved out of stone, unable or unwilling to show the emotion it needed to begin healing.

I spent time with him, going to counseling sessions and taking him out to ball games and letting him spend time with us. He seemed to have grown stronger, but he'd always been difficult to read.

"I ... didn't expect you to say that," I said. "How?"

"David was killed in the line of duty."

"How?"

"Somebody stabbed him. It happened in the field, in a hospital in Utah."

"He should have been in a classroom. Not out in the field."

"I know. But he was getting bored and asked for a transfer and I granted it."

"What happened?"

"He was there on a double homicide and was hurt. He had to be hospitalized. He must've been close 'cause the son of a bitch snuck into the hospital and killed him. And a nurse that was there with him. I have agents from the Salt Lake field office in Heber right now. They've been there two weeks and haven't turned up shit. That's when I thought of you."

"Hospitals have cameras," I said. Clearly, the FBI had thought of that but my mind was a soft mess and I couldn't organize my thoughts enough to be coherent.

"Nothing on the cameras. Wore gloves and long sleeves with jeans and a mask, like a Halloween mask."

"Murder weapon?"

"Taken with. No DNA obviously. Not even boot prints on the linoleum. He cleaned those up." A pause. "Anyway, the reason I called, I know how much David respected your work. He always told me you were the best he'd ever seen at what we do. I was wondering if you could go out to Heber and have a look?"

"A look at what?"

"I don't know. Just have a look. I'm authorizing the agents I have there for another month and then I'm sending down a few more for another month after that. Then, if we don't have anything, we'll be forced to close up shop. It'll be an open-unsolved file for a few years and then get archived and that's it. I know it's one of our own, and I'm going to fight for as long as I can, but I don't call the shots. Terrorism is eating up our resources. I wanted to try and reach out to you first. I thought David deserved that at least."

I couldn't speak. My mouth opened but nothing came out.

"Can I send you the initial police reports? Take a look at that and the autopsy and tell me what you think. If you don't think you can help, don't come out."

"Yeah. Yeah, email them to me."

"Okay, I'll get those out right away. And Jon... thanks."

"Yeah."

I hung up, my eyes not leaving the ocean. I heard rustling behind me and turned to see Emma standing at the sliding glass doors with her arms folded, staring at me. She turned without a word and went inside.

4

I went inside and saw Emma in front of the television, watching a game show with her arms still folded. I sat next to her but didn't say anything. The game show was torturing people in exchange for money. I was familiar with studies done on recruiting agents for these types of shows and reality television. They purposely looked for people suffering from mental illness. *High functioning crazies*, one television executive had called them. He explained that they made for the best television and they were just giving the public what they wanted.

"You're going, aren't you?" she said.

"He's sending me the reports. I'm going to have a look and see if I can help."

She was quiet a long time.

"You never talked about him. Who was he?"

"A really old friend that helped me out when I needed. Our families used to go on vacation together. That seems like a different lifetime now."

"Jon...."

"I know. I'm sorry."

She didn't say anything for a while and then got up and went into the bathroom and I heard the shower running. My phone buzzed and I saw I'd received a new email. Going to the Mac on my desk in the corner of the living room, I opened it.

The police reports were barely three pages in length. Three pages for the life of someone who'd hunted monsters so the rest of the world could sleep at night. The reports were terribly written, filled with misspellings and incorrect usage of forensic terms. I skimmed them and went to the reports by the special agents in the Salt Lake field office. I found nearly twenty pages of drawings, analysis, graphs, summaries, narratives and a preliminary blood report showing higher than therapeutic levels of hydrocodone in his system.

I looked at the photographs. They were high definition and color. David was laying facedown on the linoleum, a pool of congealed blood around his head like a crimson halo. His hands and shirt and pants were soaked with it. It had taken nearly twenty-five minutes for a staff member to come upon the carnage.

Both the nurse and David had died the same way: a slice across the throat, deep enough to sever the carotid artery.

Looking at his blank face, his eyes glossed over, his mouth open with a dry, lifeless tongue hanging out of the side of his mouth, I thought he looked like a deer that had just been slaughtered. My uncle had taken me hunting once and forced me to kill a deer even though I didn't want to, and it'd had the same expression on its face.

Though the special agents had done a great job, there was almost nothing to go on. The person who did this left nothing behind, and the only witness was killed as well. It was brilliant in its calculation. At that time of night the staff would be sparse. He'd gone in knowing he would kill anyone else that was there, though he probably didn't know how many people that would be.

He had to have brought a gun, too. There were too many unknowns and he couldn't be certain he wouldn't need it.

The image of David on the floor came back to me and tugged at my guts. He was one of the best friends I'd ever had and a good mentor. I pictured me retired and fishing with him on his boat. Not deciding whether to help find the man that killed him.

I was lost a moment and only the sound of the shower turning off and the frosted glass door opening brought me back. I closed the reports and went out onto the patio. The sun was still a few hours away from setting and I watched a ship out on the horizon. Pleasure yacht it looked like, white with black lettering. I kept my eyes on it and tried to follow the imperceptible movement as it slowly glided on the sea far away from shore.

Was Emma right? Could you not change who you were? Modern research suggested that change is possible to a certain age.

As a child and teenager and young adult, your core personality is malleable. But when you hit thirty that flexibility disappears and you're left with who you are. I was a homicide detective at thirty working seventy-hour weeks. The thought that that was who I was now, stuck frozen in a snapshot of my life, filled me with a cold fear that the warmth of the sun couldn't touch.

"Jon?"

"Yeah?" I said, looking behind me.

"I'm going out for a while with Rebecca. Shopping and dinner. Are you going to be here when I get back?"

I looked to the ocean again. "No."

5

I took a red-eye from Honolulu International to LAX with a one hour layover. I sat in the terminal and sipped Diet Coke to stay awake and sent a text to Emma letting her know that I loved her and would be back soon. She didn't respond. And I didn't blame her.

We had moved to Hawaii to get away from this. To get away from death and blood and thinking that led me down dark pathways. She knew, somehow, how the thinking affected me and she hated it. She didn't want to be around it. I didn't want to be around it either but I didn't have a choice. Sometimes it would overtake me.

Once, I was at a crime scene and the next thing I knew I was back home in bed. I had no idea how I had gotten there and asked my wife several times if she had driven me or if someone had dropped me off. I thought I had suffered a head injury or maybe had taken some narcotics I shouldn't have, but there was nothing like that. Part of my life had simply slipped away. The thinking had overtaken me and everything else turned to a blur.

The flight into Salt Lake City was quick, and when I stepped off the plane to the terminal a sense of icy fear touched my stomach and made me queasy. I went to the snack shop and bought some Tums and took three before going upstairs and retrieving my bag and renting a car. The clerk was an older Indian man who didn't look me in the eyes. I could tell he had taken the nightshift very purposely, attempting to get away from the interactions with people which would invariably come with the day. He handed me my keys and papers and said that someone would bring the car around front.

I went out and the night air was cool and the sky was clear and a half moon hung there like someone had taken a bite out of it. I'd lived in Utah for college and visited many times. As a Mormon, it held a special fascination for me to think of those pioneers trekking across frozen tundras to get away from the executions and the rapes.

Governor Lilburn Boggs of Missouri issued the Missouri Executive Order 44 in 1838. It was an extermination order, stating that Mormons were enemies of the state and could lawfully be executed on sight. Their women were raped and the children beaten to within an inch of their lives, if they were lucky. The men were usually hung or shot.

It was a classic tactic of tyranny: create an *us* and *them* and the mind can repress any outrage committed against the *them*. What people never realized was that the *us* became *them* arbitrarily and the torturers routinely became the tortured.

Reports from Stalin's gulags surfaced after the Cold War that torturers would burst into tears during the torture of a prisoner, exclaiming that, "It's you now, but it'll be me next." Infringing on the human rights of others always led to a loss of one's own human rights. You couldn't hurt someone else without hurting yourself. But people, it seemed, rarely learned from the past.

The car, a white Dodge Ram truck, came to the curb and a young man had me sign a release stating that I didn't see any damage anywhere. I signed it without reading and got in.

Heber was a good drive away and I thought about renting a hotel room somewhere and making the drive in the morning, but I wanted to go to the hospital now. David had been killed at three in the morning and that's how I wanted to see the hospital. How *he* had seen it.

The bright lights of downtown Salt Lake City soon turned to the dark canyons of Summit County. The air was unlike anywhere else I had been. It was cold and clean, refreshing, and I wondered just how odd it was that I should marvel at fresh air.

The road widened and narrowed sporadically and as I got off the exit and began winding down the mountain I had just climbed, I could see Heber. Few lights as it was a minor city, and because of this the surrounding forests looked like they were about to swallow it up and wipe it from existence.

I descended into the city at nearly 3:30 A.M. and found the hospital not far from Main Street. I parked out front and waited.

It was quiet, the monotony of sound broken only occasionally by the hum of an engine on the street. The hospital itself was nearly empty. I could see through the glass entrance to the emergency room and the one security guard, probably posted only after this incident occurred, was falling asleep with his feet up on the desk.

At nearly four in the morning, I got out of the truck and walked to the front entrance. I stood there a long time before going in. I could see *him* looking here. Feeling the prickly sensation of excitement and fear.

My prey is upstairs on the second floor and there's no one here to stop me.

I walked past the security guard. His head is tilted back and he's so fast asleep that he doesn't even notice me.

I get to the elevators. I make sure my gloves are on even though there are so many prints everywhere that it will be impossible to distinguish mine. Still, I want to be careful.

I go up to the second floor and wait a moment before stepping off. I'm listening to see how many people are here. I get off and walk to the desk and there's only one nurse on duty. I walk right around the desk and take her from behind. The knife gashes across her throat and I fling her down, standing over her to make sure she's not getting back up.

I hurry down the corridor, glancing into each room. And there, to my surprise, is David. He's not in a room. He's out in the hall.

I hide just off to the side so my prey can't see me. David walks out. I jump and grab him and see that he's much stronger than the nurse. We fight but I slash him. I slash him again and again in the back and he goes down.

I want to savor this. I want to take my time. So I walk up quietly and bend down over him. I lift up his head like a deer and I can't help myself, I have to see his eyes. I look down into them and the fear of death is there. It's there for everyone at this moment, no matter how tough or how many times they've been in life threatening situations. This moment is the great equalizer of us all.

I rip his throat open, so deep that a spatter of blood goes flying over the desks and papers of the nurse's station. I don't care. There's no one here to see it anyway.

I stand over him and watch as he bleeds out. And then I turn and leave.

"Hey!"

My heart jumped into my throat and I turned around to see the security guard.

"What the fuck are you doing up here?" he shouts.

"I was asked to come out here."

"Asked by who?"

"I'm helping with the investigation into David Lines' death."

"Lemme see some ID."

I pull out my wallet and hand it to him. He takes the driver license. "Don't move, I'm callin' the sheriff."

6

Everything was more difficult at night. And trying to sort out that I was actually here to help was no exception. The sheriff, who was roused from sleep only after a half hour of constant calls, had to call down to the Salt Lake field office for the FBI to verify who I was, but no one was available at four in the morning. She then had to call the main line at Behavioral Science and get someone to wake one of the special agents to verify my identity.

The entire process took two and a half hours and the sun had risen by the time I met the sheriff.

She walked in to the little security room I was being held in. Attractive and middle-aged, she wore her workout clothes and must have been going to the gym as she wasn't sweating yet. I could see the muscles in her shoulders ripple, and her calves were tight and firm.

"You caused quite a stir," she said.

"Sorry. I was going to call you but it was late."

"So you come wandering up to the site of a murder and don't think security might have a problem with that? What kinda jackass are you?"

"David was my friend. I'm here to help."

She exhaled and sat down across from me. "Sorry. I've been up since four trying to sort this out. Your buddies from the FBI are coming up later today."

"Am I free to leave?"

"Where you going?"

"Some breakfast sounded good."

"Well," she said, standing, "you might as well take me too. And you're buyin' for getting me up so early."

We sat at a café on Main Street and I ordered hash browns with eggs and an orange juice.

"They got some'a the best ham in the state up here," she said.

"I'm trying to cut back on my meat. My fiancé thinks I'm going to get high blood pressure."

"I've never met a cop that doesn't have high blood pressure."

"I'm not a cop anymore."

She leaned back in the seat. "So the FBI people said you were some consultant. You must be pretty special to be the expert the FBI calls when they need help."

"I was just his friend and he trusted me."

"You know, not three weeks ago, I sat in this very café with him and we talked. I liked him."

"He was a good man."

"He never told me how ... well, how his wife died."

I took a bite of hash browns and didn't say anything. "I haven't seen the reports from the initial investigation that he was out here on."

"Tiffany and her boyfriend?"

I nodded.

"Why do you want those?"

"Because that's how we're going to find *him*."

"The person that killed David? Wouldn't it be better to investigate his actual murder?"

"In this person's mind, this was a necessary killing. He felt David was too close to him. This killing wasn't what he needed. It's not an expression of himself. Tiffany Ochoa's killing is the purest expression we have of his unconscious. That's how we're going to find him."

"An expression of his unconscious? You think he's some sort of artist?"

I nodded. "In some ways it's the same thing. It's the same mechanism in the brain. A painter leaves things in his art that he doesn't want there. That he doesn't want to show the world. But he can't help it because, at least with good painters, it's the unconscious that's doing the work and it chooses what it wants and doesn't want. It's the same thing with the man we're after. He's left something of himself behind that he didn't want to. We just need to find what it is."

She was quiet a moment. I let the eggs run over the hash browns and dipped a forkful in ketchup before taking another bite.

"The FBI guys have a room set up at my office. You should probably see it."

7

I stood in the little storeroom at the back of the Wasatch County Sheriff's Office and stared at the photographs on the wall. They lined the room in a circle and hung above two desks that were cluttered with papers. I saw the autopsy reports for both victims and David, and several supplemental narrative reports that I hadn't received. They were laid out on desks the way I used to lay out flashcards to study in college.

The sheriff left the door open behind me and I closed it. I pulled out a chair and sat in the middle of the room and stared at the photos. Glossy and large, full of vivid color with black blood and choppy, red organs.

The girl would have been pretty, extraordinarily so, except for the thick black ooze stuck to her chin, seepage from the wound in her mouth where her tongue had been cut out. She was nude, her legs were spread, and a branch, about three feet in length with sharp edges and leaves, was thrust into her vagina. It had gone in so far it ruptured her birth canal. It was sticking out like some macabre ornament and the ground underneath it was caked in blood.

I saw him standing there, raping her with it. The more she screamed the harder he thrusted. That's what it was about. That's why he didn't kill her quickly, why he used a branch. The screams. They made him laugh several times but he couldn't tell if the laughs were from joy or pain or pleasure. He was sexually excited, but he didn't rape her himself. No semen was found anywhere in the scene. Pubic hair and latex burns were found, but not from rape. That was purposeful. He wanted me to think he could rape her. That he was able to perform.

This wasn't for sex: it was for the screams. So why cut out her tongue?

I saw him as he watched her blood in the moonlight. Blood appears as black as oil under the moon. This fascinated him. It explained many things to him. That something wasn't what it always appeared and all you had to do was change the context and it was something else.

He wouldn't be able to resist taking a part of her with him. The fingers were cut off according to the autopsy report. Would he keep them as trophies? Strip the flesh and make a necklace of the bones? Maybe. But no ... that's not what it was. That was too public. He didn't want public. This death occurred in the woods away from the public. He wanted something private, something permanent that was just between the two of them, something that would mean she was always a part of him.

He ate them.

"You must be Jon."

I snapped out and for a moment, forgot where I was. I saw a young woman, maybe thirty, standing at the doorway. She wore a suit and had an FBI badge dangling from a blue lanyard. Her hair was dirty blonde and she was smiling at me.

"Yeah," I said, swallowing, "yes. I'm Jon Stanton."

She walked toward me and held out her hand. I shook it and it was smooth with lotion. "Melissa Harding."

"Nice to meet you."

"You too. Kyle talked you up quite a bit."

A man came in behind her, also wearing a suit and an FBI badge. His hands were in his pockets and he stood behind her and looked at me. He didn't say hello and didn't stick out his hand.

"This the guy?" he said.

"This is Adam. Don't mind him," Melissa said, "he just lost a hundred bucks on a Lakers game."

"So you're the guy who's going to solve this mess, huh?"

"No," I said calmly. "No I'm not here for that. I'm just here to look at evidence and see if I can help. David was my friend."

"He was my friend too. One of the best agents I ever worked with. And you know what? When I asked for agents to swarm this little town so we can find who killed him, you know what Kyle told me? He said they didn't have the funds for it. So instead they flew out a rent-a-cop."

"I'm sorry you feel that way," I said. I didn't have the stomach for confrontation right now. I felt queasy and weak and wanted to take out the package of Tums in my pocket, but I resisted and instead stood up and placed the chair back under the desk.

"Adam, why don't you grab us some coffee?"

"They don't have any here."

"I know, just run up the street. It's not far."

He looked to me and to her and rolled his eyes as he walked out.

"Sorry," she said. "He's taking this kinda hard."

"You have nothing to apologize for. I'm the outsider. I wouldn't have come except I felt I owed it to David. He helped me on something when no one else would."

"He helped a lot of people. Even me."

I looked up to the photographs on the wall. "He had his problems, but he was a good man."

"So," she said, glancing up to the photos, "you ready to dig in? David was close."

"How so?"

"He had a good profile worked up. White male, mid-twenties, unemployed or underemployed but with an above average intelligence. Either an avid hunter or some law enforcement training because of the accuracy of the shot to the first victim's face. Her boyfriend was in the car and he shot him with an arrow first before going after Tiffany. The arrow went right through the brain. David thought he did all this to humiliate her. That's why he used the branch to rape her. I think that's pretty spot-on actually."

I shook my head, not taking my eyes off the photo of Tiffany. "That's not why he did it."

"You don't think he wanted to humiliate her?"

"That wasn't his primary motivation. He would have been more public if he wanted her humiliated. He chose a quiet spot in the woods twenty miles from the nearest house or store. Especially now, it's easy for this type of sociopath to attain humiliation for his victims. There's been a surge of rapists forcing their victims to post photos on their Facebook accounts while they're raped. It's ultimate humiliation to force all their friends and family to have to see that. He didn't want humiliation."

"Then what did he want?"

"He wanted a substitute. That's what the branch was. We're looking for someone incapable of sex, at least that night. Either through injury or some sort of neurosis that won't allow it. But he thought he would be able to perform. He would have brought something with him if he was certain he wouldn't be able to do it rather than just grabbing a branch. He thought he'd be able to, but when he actually got there he wasn't. So he grabbed whatever was nearby."

She shrugged. "That's one theory I guess."

I rose and exhaled as I did so, feeling a tug of pain in my knees. I was old enough now that even getting up caused a slight bit of pain.

"I'd like to meet her parents."

8

The home was tucked away in what appeared like the back of the city. You had to wind through several neighborhoods to reach it, and Melissa, who was driving an FBI-issued sedan, only found it by using GPS. I was sitting in the backseat and Adam was in the passenger. He didn't think I noticed but he would glance back at me in the rearview.

Heber appeared like the type of place you would want to raise a family. It was small and quaint with hometown values. I could picture the high school football game being the highlight of any weekend followed by burgers and fries at the local burger joint.

But small towns always had dark underbellies. People, particularly the young, grew bored easily and would search for ways to entertain themselves. High instances of drug and alcohol abuse were rampant in small Western and Midwestern towns and the new drug of choice was methamphetamine, not marijuana, mostly for the cost and the sustained high.

With the drugs came burglaries and robberies, and with them came sexual assaults and murders. The FBI was reporting that all crime was down, but the vast majority of crimes occurred behind closed doors without anyone ever finding out. The spouse beaten nightly by an alcoholic husband, the child sexually abused by a stepfather, the housewife prostituting herself to keep up a methamphetamine addiction... these were rarely caught and prosecuted. If all crime were tallied and totaled and everyone was made aware, I'm not sure most people could sleep at night.

We parked at the curb and I watched the house a moment.

"Remember, you're not law enforcement," Adam said, "so don't hold yourself out as an officer."

I disregarded him and opened the door and stepped outside.

The warm air had the scent of pine, and though I was exhausted I felt like I had enough energy to ignore sleep.

A paved driveway led to a walkway over the lawn and to the front door. I followed Melissa and Adam. He knocked and glanced to me to make certain I wasn't, somehow, acting like law enforcement.

A woman in her forties answered. "Can I help you?"

Adam pulled out his badge. "Federal Bureau of Investigation. Do you mind if we have a minute?"

She swallowed. "Come inside," she said, visibly shaken.

We entered the home and I tagged behind. Melissa and Adam were led to the living room and sat on a couch as Mrs. Ochoa sat on a recliner. She crossed her legs and didn't allow herself to speak first. I looked to the mantle over the small fireplace. They were all photos of Tiffany at various stages of life, the last one being her high school graduation.

Adam opened up an iPad. I could see the heading on the document: WITNESS INTAKE SHEET.

"Could you please state your daughter's birthday, ma'am?"

No, this was all wrong. I could see Mrs. Ochoa closing down. The blank stare and the body language that told me she had been through this several times and it was now routine. Her mind held more knowledge than she knew, but she wouldn't, or couldn't, access it. Not with people here asking her questions, getting a read on her. It was all so formal.

"Mrs. Ochoa," I said, before she could answer, "I just want you to know that I've done hundreds of cases just like this and it's not your fault. I know it feels like it is, but you had nothing to do with this and nothing you ever did led to it. You couldn't have stopped this."

Her eyes filled with tears. She put her hand up to her mouth and her lids closed as she wept a moment. Adam looked at me with anger in his eyes.

"Why don't you go wait in the car, Jon," he said.

"Actually, I'd like to see her bedroom, if that's all right."

Mrs. Ochoa wiped away the tears. She stood up and straightened her blouse. "It's upstairs."

I followed her up, leaving the two agents on the couch. More photos in the hallway and a few on the walls leading up the stairs. I glanced to the right as we climbed. In the kitchen I could see a Bible open on the dining table.

We turned into a room and it was as I had anticipated. Parents of murder victims who still lived at home never touch the room. They leave it exactly the same as it had been the day they passed. I stepped inside.

"Mrs. Ochoa, do you think I could have a moment alone?"

She nodded. "And thank you for saying what you said. It's... it's just...."

"I know. Everything that happens to them, we take on ourselves."

She nodded and left the room, shutting the door behind her.

I sat down on her bed and took in the room. It was adult in that it was sparse with almost no decorations, but also child-like with the few decorations there were of pop stars and stickers of brand names.

I checked under the bed and then the closet and the dresser drawers. There was nothing that would indicate anyone other than a young woman out of high school lived here. But there was something here. She had been hiding something and this was the likely place she'd hid it. Whatever it was would be a link. This *thing* saw her somewhere, desired her from somewhere. And I needed to know where she had actually spent her time that he could see her, not where her parents or the sheriff thought she'd spent her time.

The air conditioning clicked on and I could hear a noise that wasn't there before. Like a bit of paper flapping in wind. I listened for it and it was coming from near the bed.

I bent down over a heating vent, lifted it up, and reached my hand in. Something felt like plastic with putty inside. I pulled it out. Marijuana in a small plastic baggie. I slipped the baggie into my pocket and replaced the vent cover.

Nothing else of note, though I searched through all the drawers for a journal. A small calendar was stuck to her mirror and I flipped through it but it was empty.

Going back down the stairs, I saw Melissa and Adam already standing by the door with Mrs. Ochoa.

"Thank you," I said.

She nodded and waited until we were on the driveway before shutting the door.

Adam got in my face as soon as it was closed. "What the hell was that?"

"Forms aren't going to help you."

"Those forms were developed by agents a helluva lot smarter than you and used in thousands of cases just like this. And you know what, we catch the sick fucks."

"I'm not some reporter, Adam. Your numbers don't trick me. Most of the sociopaths caught are caught because they screw up or because someone else turns them in. It has nothing to do with you."

He grinned. "You think you're a hotshot? I was with Detroit Homicide for six years before joining the Bureau and I knew guys like you. Academics who thought what we did was so interesting. Well lemme tell you something, hotshot, the death of the innocent is not interesting. It's not an experiment for you to run."

"Leave him alone, Adam."

He turned away from me and headed back to the car.

"Sorry, Jon."

I pulled out the baggie of marijuana. "We should have this dusted for prints."

"Is that pot?"

"She had it hid in her air vent. I don't think the cops here will send in a request to the crime lab for me. It has to be you."

"You stole evidence?"

"It's not evidence. Not yet. And her mother didn't need to know about this. She has an image in her mind of her daughter and I don't want to tarnish that in any way."

Melissa lifted the baggie at the opening and looked at it. "Whose prints are we looking for?"

"His."

9

I sat at a bench in a small park. The print dusting would have taken a week but they'd put in a special request saying it was evidence in the murder of a law enforcement officer. We would have it back by tonight.

I was poring through the reports. Unfortunately, David never kept many notes so I wasn't able to follow his line of thinking. On the autopsy report for Tiffany, he wrote, "Thumb," and nothing else. I looked at the photos of her thumbs. One had suffered trauma. He'd attempted to cut through it, and there were injuries on both sides. A pair of sharp scissors or gardening shears might have done it, but why hadn't he been able to simply cut it off?

I glanced through the boyfriend's autopsy report as well. One arrow wound from a bow or crossbow through the cheek. The round had shattered the bone, entered the skull, and severed the brain stem from the brain before exiting out of the neck. It would have to be something high-powered to do that kind of damage. Amazingly, there wasn't a ballistics report. Ballistic specialists were expensive but the state crime lab or even a bigger, neighboring city would have sent someone for free.

I took out my cell phone and dialed the number Melissa had given me as her cell.

"This is Agent Harding."

"Melissa, Jon Stanton. I had a quick question if you have a minute."

"Yeah."

"Why wasn't there a ballistics analysis done?"

"Oh, we talked to the sheriff about that. She had asked one of her deputies to call the state lab and have them send someone and he just completely forgot. By the time it was all sorted out, the family had already buried the victim."

"Does the ME still have the arrow?"

"He's given it back to the sheriff's office. David didn't really follow up because he didn't believe the boyfriend was the primary target of these murders."

"Can we get a ballistics report?" Silence on the other end. "Hey, look, I know this isn't my case and I'm not even law enforcement anymore. I'm just trying to do what I can."

"I know. And Kyle said to help you in any way we can. Sure, I think we should send it back to Quantico or have the Salt Lake County Sheriff's laboratories do it."

"What's the turnaround time in Quantico?"

"If it was involved in David's death, we'll be first."

"Okay. I appreciate that, thank you."

"Welcome."

I hung up, grateful that Melissa had been the special agent assigned. I recalled days back in Homicide when the feds would come in and bulldoze a case. They would become the pointmen for witnesses, media, laboratories, and even the victim's families. Detectives would clam up and not provide new evidence that had been uncovered and it would usually disintegrate into two separate investigations, neither helping the other.

I flipped through the rest of the report and Sheriff Cannon's notes on Dale Christensen interested me. He had been the one to find the bodies, claiming he had been dumped by friends in a nearby location and came upon them by accident. Given how far into the woods the bodies had been found, that seemed extremely improbable. He was currently held at the jail on unrelated charges.

Driving to a jail made my heart pound in my chest and I saw the rings of sweat around my underarms as I parked. Each jail was different only in architecture. The interiors were all the same. A poet I liked had once said that you knew society was crumbling when the madhouses were closed and the jails were full.

The mentally ill were not given breaks in the criminal justice system. Most of them were housed in jails or prisons and force-fed medication in an attempt to keep them docile. But without proper treatment under a psychiatric staff, they spent their lives in quiet lunacy, ruled by hallucinations and ghosts.

I stepped out and went across the parking lot to the entrance, hesitating a moment before opening the door. Walking inside, I found the check-in desk. Visiting hours were over.

"Dale Christensen, please."

"You'll have to come back in the evening after dinner."

"I'm a professional visit." I pulled out my wallet and inside was my private investigator license for California.

She glanced from the photo to my face and back before saying, "Just a minute."

It was a good twenty minutes before they were ready for me. I went through the metal detectors and was then wanded before the metal doors clicked and slid open. I stood outside them a minute, staring at the gray walls.

"You goin' or stayin'?"

I walked past the guard and inside the cell block. The corridor wasn't long and I walked slowly until I found the visitor's room. I sat down on a metal stool and behind glass sat a man who was probably in his forties but looked in his sixties. A life of hard and fast living shone on his face and revealed a heart and mind that was just as old. He was a man who was beaten down and bitter and I saw the tip of a swastika tattoo sticking out from his sleeve.

"Who the hell are you?"

"I'm Jon Stanton. I'm a friend of the FBI agent that was killed, David Lines."

He nodded. "Yeah. Nice dude. Snuck me in some cigarettes in exchange for some info."

I grinned. "That sounds like him."

"Well what'dya need?"

"I think the same person that killed Tiffany Ochoa killed David. I just wanted to go through what you remembered about that day."

"Man, I spoke with like five cops that day. Can't you just go read them reports?"

"I'd rather hear it from you."

He shrugged. "Ain't really that much to tell. I woke up near the campsite we was at. My fuckin' so called friends left me there 'cause I got loaded. I got up and started walkin'. I saw them bodies and when I got to town, I called the cops."

"What'd you see exactly?"

"The car and the dude that was in the driver seat. The girl was tied up to the tree."

"Did you see anything around? Anything on the ground?"

"Nah, nothin' like that. I saw the girl with her guts hangin' out and I walked away, man."

"Who did you speak with when you called the police?"

"I dunno, some dude."

"Did they take you back to the site?"

"Yeah, just to show 'em where it was. Then all the cops in the town came out and pulled out their yellow tape'n shit and they give me a ride home."

"What friends left you out there?"

"I dunno, man. They was barely my friends. I didn't know 'em good."

I had studied micro-facial expressions in depth in my doctorate program with an eye toward application in law enforcement. I'd even conducted a study on the seven emotions expressed through micro-expressions: anger, fear, sadness, happiness, contempt, surprise, and disgust. A professor named Ekman thought micro-expressions conveyed much more than the seven emotions and added several to the list, but the most important were guilt and shame.

Micro-expressions did not express or cover lies. That was impossible. All they did was convey an emotion the subject was attempting to conceal.

A certain percentage of the population, somewhere around three percent, are perfect liars. They show no physical manifestations when they lie and micro-facial expressions are useless with them. Sociopaths fit into this category as masters of manipulation and fraudulent behavior. They have an inability to feel any genuine emotion and it's nearly impossible to detect a concealed emotion through their micro-expressions. But the rest of the population can't help but have a slight tick or curl of the lip or a glance in another direction when they lie, attempting to hide their surprise or their guilt.

A coding system called the Facial Action Coding System or FACS was developed by a Swedish anatomist named Carl Hjortsjö and was the basis of micro-facial expression analysis. The system uses a scoring mechanism called AU, for action units, to score a subject's facial movements. In almost everything Dale told me, I saw an inner brow raise, an AU score of one, an upper lid raise, a score of five, and a stretch of the lip, a score of twenty.

Dale Christensen was lying to me.

10

I left the jail with practically no additional information but a strong sense that Dale had either killed Tiffany or knew who did. I checked the jail incarceration records before I left and he had been in custody when David was killed.

My phone rang. It was Melissa.

"Hey," I said.

"Hey. Thought you'd wanna know that we got your print results."

"That was quick."

"David had a lot of friends."

"What'd you find?"

"Three prints. Tiffany, you, and a John Doe. We ran the John Doe through IAFIS and got a hit on a Carl Velazquez in Park City."

"It must be her dealer."

"That's my guess. You wanna head up there with me?"

"Sure. I'm in the parking lot of the jail."

"I'll swing by right now."

"Actually, I haven't rented a room yet. There's a Motel 6 down the block. Can you meet me there?"

"Yup. See you in a jiff."

I hung up and got in the car and pulled out of the Justice Complex onto Main Street. I could see the big blue sign for Motel 6 and I drove there. It was rundown but I'd stayed in worse. I pulled to the front and went inside. A man was behind the counter with a permanent grimace on his face as he watched a daytime soap on a little color television behind the counter.

"Thirty-five a night or ninety a week," he said without looking at me.

"Let's do a week." I pulled out my credit card and handed it to him. He ran it, printed the receipt and a user agreement without taking his eyes off the television.

Once I was checked in, I went to the room on the second floor. I opened the door and went inside and was surprised that it was actually clean with fresh sheets on the bed that smelled like they'd just come out of a dryer. I sat down on the bed and took off my shoes and lay back, staring at the ceiling. My head was pounding and I wished I'd purchased some ibuprofen as well as the Tums yesterday.

I took out my cell phone and dialed my ex-wife's number, realizing that Agent Harding and my ex had the same first name. Even though it was inconsequential, I don't know why I didn't recognize it earlier.

"Hi Jon."

"Hi. How's Boston?"

"Cold as hell. How are you doing? Matt said you're living in Honolulu now?"

"Yeah, we bought a little place."

"You and the professor, huh?"

"Yeah," I said.

I could sense the hostility in her voice. Melissa had been stunningly beautiful all her life, and like many gorgeous women, had never had to worry about her intellect, assuming that her looks would carry her through the rest of her life. As she found that looks, and the splendor they brought, faded with time, she grew bitter she hadn't developed her intellect and was now beholden to men for her style of life. She had a degree but little career history and her husband was her sole source of support. I gladly would have supported her if she needed, but she didn't know that and had never bothered to ask.

"The kids are out. I'll tell them you called."

"Jon Junior asked me something the other day."

"What?"

I hesitated. "He asked if he could come live with me."

The line went silent a long time.

"And what did you tell him?"

"I told him I would speak with you."

"He's too young. And I don't want to split them apart."

"Is something going on?"

"Like what?"

"I don't know," I said. "Something that would upset him?"

A sound came through like plastic against skin; she was chewing on her lower lip, which she only did when stressed. "He's not doing well with my new marriage. He keeps saying that he thinks it's my fault we divorced and that his father doesn't live with us because of me."

"He's just angry. He was angry with me at first and now he's angry with you. It's natural."

"It doesn't feel natural. He's ten and he told me he doesn't have an emotional connection with me. What ten year old even knows what an emotional connection is, Jon?"

"He's always been perceptive. But... I don't think it would be a bad idea for him to come out. At least for a little while, and see what it's like."

"You can't be serious. With the life you lead?"

"I'm not a cop anymore, Mel. I'm not even a PI. I just teach at the University and come home. Nine to five."

"Maybe you can fool your new wifey with that, Jon, but I know you. I know what you're like. You have darkness in you. You've managed to control it and put it to good use, but it's still there and it follows you around. It brings wickedness into your life. I don't want my children around that. Not ever again."

"I can't respond to anything you've said. You make accusations that are unverifiable. And what I used to do has no bearing on what I am now." I knew this was a lie. What frightened me was how correct she was in her assessment of me. Summing me up in just a few sentences. *A darkness in me that brought wickedness.* Would the darkness affect Emma too? Would it affect everyone who came near me like some plague?

"I don't want him living with you. It's too dangerous."

I heard honking out in the parking lot. "I have to go. We'll talk more later."

"Whatever."

I hung up and went to the window and saw Melissa in the driver's seat of a silver sedan. Stepping outside, I saw the man in the room next door come out, too. He leaned over the railing and stared down at her but didn't say anything.

"Hey," I said, getting into the passenger seat.

"Hey."

We pulled out onto Main Street and began heading to Park City.

THOMAS FISCHER

"Thomas?" she yelled out from behind me. I ignored her.

I sat at the laptop out on my balcony overlooking Park City and read about Jon Stanton. The man the media said was called out by the FBI to help in the murder investigation of Tiffany Ochoa.

I was curious who the FBI turned to when they needed help. That's how a local crime blog described him: the FBI's go-to guy. He was… interesting.

He held the record for the most officer-involved shootings at the San Diego Police Department. Several websites claimed he was a psychic and that he'd provided clues and proof of his supernatural prowess throughout the years. He had a higher clearance rate on murder cases than any other detective in the police department's history, and one blog claimed, in essence, that it takes one to know one. How delightful that was.

One of the most interesting bits was that a former partner of his, Eli Sherman, had tried to kill him after Stanton discovered that he'd been murdering young women, using his badge to pick them up. Sherman escaped custody and was still on the loose. How stimulating it would be to meet him.

I read a few more blog posts, most of them discussing the beautifully gory details of various cases he had handled, and then closed the laptop and sipped my whiskey as I looked over the city below me. I had no neighbors and was surrounded exclusively by pine trees on the slope of a mountain. The parcel had cost me quite handsomely, but what was money for after all.

"Thomas," the woman said behind me again, "are you coming back to bed?"

I looked up to the setting sun that was blood-red and the pink clouds burnt by its glory and grinned to myself. How fortunate she was. Not just to be with me, but that I did not have any urges currently other than base sexual ones.

I rose and went inside and grabbed her by the hair, kissing her hard and biting her lip. She was wearing a pink robe and her blonde hair danced on her shoulders. I held on to it as I spun her around and bent her over my desk. I spanked her several times and she yelped with pleasure. I lowered my pants to my knees and lifted her robe over her waist, revealing a perfect ass. I did nothing at first, simply admiring it, before leaning down and biting it.

I then entered her and thrust violently. So much so that she began telling me to slow down and go easy. When she did this, I would thrust harder and slap the back of her head. At one point she began to cry.

When I was finished, I went to the bathroom and threw a towel to her and it hit her in the face. Her humiliation was so palpable that I couldn't move. It was mesmerizing. She looked at me as she dressed and headed out the door. She feigned anger but she would be back if I called her. I would need a few simple words and she would be back. How odd it was that women always believed apologies.

After a shower, I dressed in black slacks with loafers and no socks, a blue button-down shirt and gold cufflinks. I had a party of sorts to attend and a date I was excited about. I regretted now having intercourse beforehand as I wasn't as motivated, but I knew I would be able to perform again shortly.

I checked my Mariner Rolex, which revealed I had an hour until I was meeting my date. I went down the stairs to the basement. The door was locked and I used a key to get in and locked it behind me.

It was pitch-black, a type of darkness that was rare, someplace that no light penetrated, not even a crack underneath the door. I pressed my hand to the wall and gingerly felt around before flipping a switch and flooding the room with lights.

Carpeted white and with a bearskin rug with fine wood furniture, it was a sanctuary. I had read somewhere that Jack Kennedy had such a room, a reprieve from the world in which he only brought those who were worthy to enter.

I sat down at my desk and glared at the wall a moment. I then reached into a drawer and came up with several large, glossy photos and spread them on the desk before me. Tiffany Ochoa was weeping as I cut her. In one photo, she was looking directly into the camera and I stared at her for a long while.

How foolish I was not to film the scene. I could still hear her screams in my ears and they were like candy. They had flavors, textures. And I hadn't thought to preserve it.

This was my first. I would correct it next time.

JON STANTON

As Melissa and I drove down the mountain to Park City, I noticed that her nails were chewed down to her fingers. At the base were flecks of color and I knew she attempted not to bite down on them but couldn't stop.

"So," she said, "you think the dealer had something to do with it?"

"No, not really. I just want to see what he knows."

"He's as likely a suspect as anyone else."

"I don't think so. Not for this type of offense. We're looking for someone with specific traits. Tiffany was chosen, she wasn't random or desired just because she happened to be nearby."

"Who do you picture when you see her killer?"

"White male, thirties, no history of sexual offenses. He's too intelligent to be caught for the minor ones. But as a juvenile he may have racked up some voyeurism charges. Peeping into neighbor's windows at night, things like that. Probably arrested or caught at school with violent pornography as well."

"Intelligent, huh? David thought he was disorganized and careless."

"No, this was purposeful. Everything about it was purposeful. I don't think he's sloppy except for one detail and that's the arrow. He could have dug that out and deprived us of it. But he didn't. I think he might have been interrupted or gotten frightened and finished earlier than he anticipated. And I think the initial profile was wrong about his being an underachiever. Someone with these types of impulses that goes his entire life without acting on them until now has incredible self-control. There's a well-established correlation between self-control and intelligence, as well as social and financial success. I think we're looking for someone that's probably a professional of some kind."

"That's assuming you're right about this being the first time for him."

"He didn't cut through the thumb, though he wanted to. He was rushed somehow. Something wasn't anticipated and he ran. That's panic. As a sociopath like this progresses in his ritual, he panics less and less and is calmer and more collected. This one had mistakes caused by alarm. He'll correct his behavior next time."

She was silent a moment. "We don't have Behavioral Science in this field office. I work fraud cases, primarily mortgage fraud." She looked to me, embarrassed, but I showed no reaction. "I've always been fascinated by what the agents in the BSU do, working with sociopaths. I looked you up online. From what I could tell you've made a career chasing them."

"A small percentage of them. Most sociopaths are actually high functioning. They're likely to be CEO's and politicians and doctors and lawyers. A CMO I profiled once during graduate school was known as the Terminator. He enjoyed going into a town and firing twenty-five percent of the staff at factories and plants. He would joke with them as he did it as people cried in his office. He couldn't relate to the emotions he was seeing and he found them humorous.

"That's *most* sociopaths. There's a disconnect between their amygdala and frontal cortex that prevents them from feeling empathy. The type I used to chase, and probably the type that killed Tiffany, is a sexual sadist, the most dangerous type of sociopath. He has the amygdala dysfunction of the typical sociopath but violence and sex have become linked in his mind, and unless his sexual partner is feeling some sort of pain or humiliation, he won't be able to climax. But it takes a while for that connection to solidify. He'll daydream about the violence, sometimes for years, and when it finally happens it'll overwhelm him at first. That's why I don't think he could perform with Tiffany. I think her sheer terror surprised him and impotence followed. But he's daydreaming about it now, and it arouses him. He wants to experience it again and this time he will be able to perform. And it'll be more vicious."

She took a deep breath. "Wow. I'm kind of glad I didn't get assigned to BSU."

I grinned, though I didn't find it funny. "My first assignment in law enforcement was the DUI squad in San Diego. And I was happy to be there. When I was made detective I thought about the major cases I'd be working, the types of people I would deal with that most of society doesn't know exist among them. That seems like a lifetime ago now."

"I'm sorry about the way Adam treats you. It's not fair."

"He's just scared."

"Of what?"

"That what happened to David could happen to him. Federal agents are the elite of the elite in law enforcement and to think that your badge and gun and the power of the federal government can't protect you from a single cracked person is terrifying."

"Yeah," she said absently.

I looked to her. "Sorry, I didn't mean—"

"No, you're right. It really frightened me when I heard about David. You don't hear about federal agents dying very often unless it's overseas. And to think it happened in a hospital with thirty people inside…"

The trees were a lush green and the street was wide with canyons and streams on either side. The rushing water was pleasant to listen to and I rolled down my window the entire length and stuck out my arm and let the wind hit me.

Park City was small, but the most expensive place to live in Utah, even though the homes varied from colossal mansions in Jeremy Ranch to small shacks filled with ten people near Main Street. The city council had banned billboards and it added a beauty to the scenery that was difficult to find in most states. The only comparable places I had been to were Ketchum and Sun Valley, Idaho. But the fact that Hemingway killed himself there always gave it a darker tone.

We came in through a back road and past Park City High School, turned left toward Main Street and the GPS led us to a series of condominiums tucked away behind some older homes. Parking was difficult so we went across the road and parked in the stall of a city government building.

We crossed the street and went past the homes to the condos. Melissa got a phone call from Adam, who was in Salt Lake at the crime lab following up on the prints and rushing the ballistics through. She spoke curtly in "yes" and "no" answers and hung up without saying goodbye.

"I'm guessing he had a few words to say about me."

She glanced back to me. "He told Kyle he could handle this and Kyle told him he couldn't, that he was bringing in an expert. David was Adam's ASAC when Adam first started with the Bureau."

We went up a path between several condos and came to the address listed in the GPS on her phone. The condo was light blue with a small white porch. A table sat in front with a few chairs and two ashtrays filled with cigarette butts. One of the butts had lipstick on it and I stared at it for longer than I should have. The red glistened and the smears appeared like blood sliding down the side of the brown tube.

"You okay?"

"Yeah," I said. "Sorry. Did you knock?"

"Yeah. No answer."

I took a few steps back and looked into the upstairs window. I saw movement, as if someone had been peeking out through the blinds and then pulled away.

"FBI," Melissa shouted. "If you do not open the door I will be forced to apply for a warrant and come back with SWAT."

Melissa looked to me and grinned.

A few moments later the door opened and a skinny man with red-rimmed eyes stood at the door. He was wearing a blue tank-top and a silver chain dangled from his neck into a puff of blond chest hair.

Melissa pulled out her badge and flashed it before replacing it. "We need to ask you some questions about Tiffany Ochoa."

The man's eyes went wide. "I don't know who dat is."

"Fine," she said, "you're under arrest for the murder of Tiffany Ochoa." She grabbed his wrist and spun him around. "You have the right to remain silent, anything you say—"

"Yo! Murder! What! I ain't done nothin', man. I ain't done nothin'."

"You're not being honest with us. It's easier to just arrest you and deal with you at the station."

"Nah, man. I'm on parole, man. Don't do me like this."

Melissa let him go. I asked him, "What're you on parole for?"

"Burglary, man."

"Then tell us the truth and this visit stays between us," I said. "You sold weed to Tiffany Ochoa. How often did you do it?"

"Couple times a month, man. Nothin' big."

"How did you know her?"

"We went to high school together."

I paused. "You heard she died, right?"

"Yeah, I heard, man. And it sucks. She was a good chick."

"Did she have any enemies that you knew of?" Melissa asked.

"Nah, she wasn't like that. She was cool. Everybody liked her, you know."

"When was the last time you saw her?" I asked.

"Few weeks ago, man. She bought a dime-bag from me."

"Was she into harder drugs?"

"Nah, man. Not if you in Heber. You wanna just chill, you don't wanna be all tweeked out'n shit. People'll know."

I glanced back to the cigarette with the lipstick. It was in the middle of the ashtray with several others on top of it, suffocating it. Black-gray ash dotted the table and the cement underneath. A few cigarette burns were on the cushions of the chairs.

"I saw her closet. She had nice clothes."

"What?" he said.

I looked to him. "She had a lot of nice clothing. But our information says she was unemployed. Was she working for you?"

"She wasn't like that. She wouldn't ever sell to nobody 'cause she'd feel bad if they got hurt or somethin'. She worked as a waitress, under the table'n shit. Didn't have no papers."

"Waitress where?"

"Café right here, man. Café Lemon. It's down on Main."

I looked to Melissa, gesturing if she had anything else.

"Don't leave town."

"I can't," he said. He put his leg out and revealed a blinking ankle monitor.

"What do you think?" she asked, when we were back in the car.

"He's telling the truth. I need to go to that café."

"I'll head down."

"I'd like to go by myself if that's okay."

"Oh. Sure. I guess."

"I'm about to confront her employer and reveal that he's a tax cheat. I think it'd be better alone without law enforcement there."

2

Café Lemon was on the corner of the western entrance to Main Street in Park City across from an art gallery. I had to park up the street and paralleled between a truck and an Escalade. I got out and felt the afternoon sunshine on my face and stood for a while and breathed the clean air.

Walking down the main strip, I glanced into the various shops. I passed a new age store that advertised for in-house psychic readings and an ice cream parlor with a 1950s style soda fountain behind the counter. Intermingled with the quaint and small was the luxurious, stores where a single shirt cost over nine hundred dollars and a suit could run into the tens of thousands.

Park City was a town centered on one event: the Sundance Film Festival. Any other time it was quiet and had a small-town charm. But during Sundance movie stars and rock stars and porno queens and writers and directors and poets would descend and turn the city inside out. Nightclubs and bars that didn't exist during the rest of the year would open up, parties would occur every night, and the streets would be mobbed with tourists and locals trying to hob-nob with celebrity. As if a chance encounter in the street were a story they could tell their children years later.

I had gone once and it was overwhelming, the noise and the crowds and the desperation hanging in the air. I left early after watching only one film about a disturbed filmmaker who was attempting to document his slipping sanity with a film crew following him around at every moment of his life.

Several cars sped by and didn't stop for me. I waited until it was clear and sprinted across the street as a red Lexus nearly clipped me.

The café was dimly lit and smelled of coffee and pastries. It appeared more like a coffee shop that happened to serve food than a restaurant. The space held a lot of bookshelves overflowing with paperbacks and the walls were lined with soft recliners and fake leather couches. The hostess was flirting with one of the waiters since there was only one couple and a single man seated in the entire place. She saw me and came over, smiling at the last possible moment and saying, "Hi, how many in your party?"

"Just one."

She sat me in the back near the kitchen and I had a view of the entire café. A bar was on the far side with a bartender in a black vest and white long-sleeved shirt. He was cleaning the bar and stocking liquors and checking the napkins and straws. At the other end of the café was a lone man in a sports coat with a laptop open and stacks of cash that he appeared to be cataloguing.

"Hi," the waiter said, "my name is Richard and I'll be taking care of you today. Our menu is mostly soups and sandwiches but our pastries are made fresh every morning by Chef Joshua."

"Just a grilled cheese if you have it."

"We don't, unfortunately. We have primarily artisan sandwiches but we can probably get you one of our sandwiches without the meat."

"That's fine."

"Great, and did you want a side salad with that?"

"No, and just water to drink. Thanks. One question, though: is that the manager over there?"

"Oh, that's the owner but, yeah, he manages the place too."

"Great. Thanks."

"No problem. Your food will be out in a minute."

I waited until he left and then stood and walked across the restaurant. I sat across from the owner and his brow furrowed.

"That seat's taken."

"I just had a quick question for you," I said. "Did Tiffany's parents know she was working under the table for you?"

The man froze. It would have almost been comical if it wasn't the context it was.

"I'm not with the IRS and I don't really care that you were paying her under the table. I'm trying to find the man that killed her."

"So, hypothetically, if I did employ her, what would that have to do with anything?"

"I don't know. I just want to rule everything out."

"Are you a police officer?"

"No."

"Well, then I don't have to talk to you, do I?"

"No. But if it matters you don't have to talk to the actual police either."

"I think I'd like you to leave."

"There's no reason for her to work under the table, is there? She wasn't a felon, so it wouldn't be against policy to hire her, and she was able and capable of working. She could have worked part time and you'd avoid benefits… It's funny, I just can't imagine why an owner would risk federal tax fraud charges just for one employee? Can you?"

He glared at me and I held his gaze. I didn't need to say anything. Silence was often the most effective form of questioning.

Whatever they had going on was implied and I could actually know or be bluffing, but he wouldn't know. The question was, would he risk it?

"What do you want to know?" he said evenly.

"She didn't have a car. Was it her boyfriend that picked her up every day?"

"She didn't work every day. She just worked Fridays and Saturdays. And yeah, it was her boyfriend that would come and get her."

"Did she ever say anything to you about being afraid of someone? Maybe receiving hang-up calls or running into the same person in different places?"

He shook his head. "No, nothing like that."

"Any customers that paid her too much attention?"

"Every customer paid her too much attention. Did you see any pictures of her before… well, before all this?"

"No."

"She was a knockout. Pure and simple. I was the one that kept telling her she had to go to California and use her looks for something other than serving fat tourists ham and Brie. She was really shy though, and insecure. I don't think she saw how good-looking she was."

I thought of my own ex-wife. "They rarely do."

"Yeah," he said, tapping a pencil against the table. "So we done?"

"What was her shift?"

"Noon to four."

I nodded. "Thanks for your help."

I ate and, surprisingly, the sandwich was delicious. After I finished, I nodded to the owner as I left.

Stepping back out into the sunshine, I glanced up across the street to an office building—though the office buildings here didn't look like office buildings. They looked more like log cabins with multiple stories. At the top of the building was a sign for Helix Financial & Commodities with a simple black and white logo which didn't seem to fit the building.

Next to that building was a hotel with a ski store on the ground level. I went inside and perused and bought some sunglasses. The clerks were both condescending and rude but they certainly accepted my money quickly and without fuss. I thanked them and they didn't say anything as I left.

Today was Thursday. Tomorrow, I would be back here and sitting in the café. He had met her somewhere. The killing was too precise to be random. Somewhere, he had daydreamed about her. About the things he would do to her. And I thought this café was as good a place as any.

THOMAS FISCHER

I woke not knowing where I was. Occasionally that would happen without cause. I turned over in the bed and looked out the patio glass doors that I had left open and onto the forest that I knew surrounded my home. Nude, I rose and went out onto the patio and urinated over the side to the ground ten feet below.

The party the night before had been quite the fucking bore. People mingling forcefully, all attempting to think of something witty to say to each other, something that convinced others that they indeed had value aside from the size of their bank accounts, most of which had been inherited from parents.

My date, a brunette with short hair and wide, crimson lips, withstood the onslaught of the old rich douchebags hitting on her the entire night by having an air of insolence. I glanced over several times and saw her sipping champagne and ignoring men who were attempting with all their might to convey with a single sentence not only their ivy league educations, but the number of companies and employees they had under them.

I left her alone, careful to show her I was indifferent. At one point she came up to me and I put my arm around her waist and she pushed me off without looking at me. The bitch would pay for that.

"Can you just take me home?" she asked, after receiving a text. No doubt from the artist boyfriend I knew she had.

"Sure."

As we drove, she kissed and groped me. We stopped on the side of the road and had sex.

I dropped her off and she got out and asked if I would call her, and I said I wouldn't. I could see her boyfriend waiting on the porch. He began to yell at her. Then he ran at me.

Normally, I would have gladly broken his head open, but I was tired and glutted from sex and caviar and champagne, so I figured why bother. I drove away with him chasing me down the street, swearing and looking for something to throw. I couldn't help but laugh.

I laughed so much I couldn't stop and I had to pull over. I kept laughing until my stomach pained me so badly I had to think about something else. Something less humorous. Work. Work always seemed to take the humor out of a situation. So I thought about the various tasks that required completion the next day and soon the humor faded and I was able to drive home.

I slept in the nude with the windows open, hoping to hear the coyotes that haunted these hills at night. Black bears were frequent visitors as well, but they had developed a deep fear of humans and wouldn't come near the homes. But I would hear them grunting along their paths on the hillside.

By morning I didn't feel refreshed in any way. I'd only had dreams in black and white and they'd awoken me several times. I felt groggier than when I went to bed and thought that perhaps I would have felt better had I stayed awake the entire night.

I showered and donned an Armani suit with a pink polo shirt and black loafers with no socks. I placed a pink pocket square in the jacket pocket and slicked back my hair with a Parisian sculpting gel I'd had imported from a little store that made the gels and soaps they sold.

I chose to drive the Cheyenne and went into town. I did one loop around Main to see who was out, but it was ten in the morning and there was hardly any crowds. I parked in reserved parking at the entrance to my building and went inside.

Elevators sounded constricting, so I chose to take the stairs to the top floor, and saw the massive gleaming sign for Helix Financial & Commodities behind the receptionist's desk.

"Morning, Karen."

"Morning. How was your night?"

"As expected. How was yours?"

"Pizza and *Modern Family*. What else?"

"You should go out with me sometime. I can show you the

sights."

"The sights in Park City? I grew up here."

"No, I don't mean here. I'll take you to Vegas. That's where you go to have a good time."

"Hmm. I'll think about it."

"I'll take that as a maybe."

I walked past her through the glass doors into the main foyer. She wouldn't go out with me. She was a lesbian and thought that somehow I didn't know. So it was always enjoyable to ask her out and watch her squirm for answers. On the one hand, she didn't want to reject the CEO of the company. On the other, she felt uncomfortable telling me she was homosexual. Probably because she hadn't come out to her family yet as she was only nineteen.

I wound my way past the conference room and saw a meeting taking place. I checked the calendar on my phone: I had scheduled this meeting. Sneaking in through the back, several people turned to me and smiled and I smiled too. The lights were dimmed and Roger, one of my account managers, was going through a PowerPoint about Libya's interim government's stance on oil futures and trading with the West.

I paid attention for only a few moments before noticing Silvia's slit in her skirt. She was seated next to me, and with her eyes turned toward Roger, didn't notice that I was looking. Her legs were smooth and white with just enough tan in them not to be pale. Musculature was visible in both calves and thighs and her ankles were pronounced with a single vein coming around them. They were perfect.

She glanced over at me and grinned awkwardly and I forced a smile and she turned away.

I was still staring at her when the lights came on.

"Any questions?" Roger asked. "Okay, unless Thomas has something to add..."

I shook my head. "That was great. Thanks for that, Roger. So just a reminder we're pushing Schiller Exports this week. The price per share is reasonable but the buy-in is thirty thousand minimum. Hit your upper middle-class clients, some of your retirement funds, but don't pass this on to your big dogs. I have a feeling it's going to tumble in the next few months."

Roger looked around. "All right, let's go sell some oil."

Everyone stood and walked out. Everyone except Roger, who came and sat next to me.

"You look like shit," he said.

"Thanks."

"You take melatonin like I recommended?"

"No, I forgot to pick some up."

"It'll help. Without sleep you're more prone to disease, irritability, depression, everything."

"You don't want to talk about sleep with me, Roger. What is it you need?"

He rubbed his forehead with one hand and said, "It's Mark."

"What about him?"

"He gave me his two week notice last night. He's leaving for GE in New York."

"Why would he possibly want to live in New York?"

"Thomas, did you hear what I said? Mark is leaving. He's the best damned account rep we got."

"Why's he leaving?"

"He says you're cruel to him."

I laughed. When I saw Roger wasn't laughing as well, I stopped.

"Sorry," I said.

"Thomas, he says you tease him about everything. His clothes, his weight, his parents, his teeth... everything."

"So what? I tease Jason about being black, I tease Linda about being Muslim..."

"And you can't do that. Look, I've known you a long time and know you're one charming dude when you want to be, and one serious asshole when you want to be. Can we just have a little more charming and a little less asshole at the office?"

I put on my best fake smile. Outwardly, I was showing him he had gotten through and I'd be happy to do what I could to help. I knew he liked me, as most people did. I was the perfect friend, the perfect lover, the perfect boss. I became what they wanted to see and only once in a while would my mask slip and reveal the twisted wreckage underneath.

"For you, Roger, anything."

"I appreciate it. Thank you. Now, when we going golfing?"

"This afternoon?"

"Can't, client meetings. Tomorrow after lunch?"

"You're on."

I waited until he left before standing. My head and upper body caught in the projector's light and it cast a black shadow on the wall. It was the perfect depiction of myself: nothing on the inside. People would comment to me all the time how charming I was, how witty, how full of life. My ex-girlfriend had told me that her parents loved me more than she did. I was just the right mixture of handsome and successful and mysterious to be appealing.

But I knew the truth. I had no delusions about it. I was the shadow. I was an outline with a dark center that I could never penetrate. And because of this center I couldn't see the centers of anyone else. So I became what they showed me. When I met a person—and I'd met enough people to have a statistically valid sample of the population—I knew that no matter who they were or where they came from, they would like me.

I would become like them, sometimes unconsciously, but most of the time with an eye toward ensuring that I appeared sympathetic and agreeable. They would think of me as a friend and I wouldn't know the first thing about how they related to the world, what their hopes were, their dreams, their relationships, their inner thoughts, their motivations… human beings were all a mystery to me.

Two years ago I watched as a woman's husband drown in a pool. He hit his head and sank to the bottom and none of the lifeguards had been paying attention. The woman was hysterical and weeping uncontrollably and I couldn't figure out why. She was relatively decent looking, not ugly and not pretty. She would find another husband. What did it matter whether it was the corpse at the bottom of the pool or some other loser she found at the grocery store or gym?

It fascinated me the entire length of the day. I drove home, and as I went about my nighttime routine, I tried to mimic the sounds she'd been making, the frantic cries for someone, anyone, to do something to save her husband. It wasn't easy, but it was something that had to be perfected.

I walked out into the hall and past thirty or so cubicles and another dozen offices. Mine was the corner office with the frosted glass walls. I walked in and shut the door behind me. A remote control was on my desk and I pressed a button and the stereo mounted on the wall turned on. I opened iTunes on my computer, which was connected to the stereo, and played some Coltrane.

Just as I was relaxing in my chair with my feet up on the desk, someone knocked on the door and broke my concentration.

"What?" I said.

Char, one of our staff, poked her head in. "Mr. White is here to see you, sir."

"Tell him I'm not in."

"Um, I think he saw your car outside. He knows you're here."

"Where is he?"

"In the foyer."

"Send him back in five minutes."

She left and I sighed and turned the stereo off and exited the office. Another staff member was near my office, Alexis something, and I went to her. "Phillip White is going to go into my office and see that no one is there. When he does, tell him I went for a client meeting with someone else and won't be back until the afternoon. If he says my car is here, tell him the other person drove."

"Sure, Mr. Fischer."

I took the back door and went down the emergency exit, which was nothing more than a little winding staircase locked away next to the parking garage. It echoed loudly and with each step you grew more disoriented as you weren't exactly certain where in the descent you were.

Getting down the stairs and opening the exit door, I glanced both ways before slinking out and crossing the street. Café Lemon was there and they had the best espresso in the city. I went inside and sat down.

2

My father summoned me later that afternoon. He never requested, it was always a summons. I received a text at around one P.M. saying, *Get your ass over here.*

I went home and changed into something more conservative first. A gray suit with a gold tie and pocket square. I drove my Cadillac, and though the ride was smooth, it annoyed me. It was associated now with greasy mobsters and old men and I didn't want to be seen in it. But it was my father's favorite type of car.

I parked outside city hall in handicap parking and went inside. The space was decorated with flags and paintings of veterans, a statue of Brigham Young up in the corner that was slated to be taken down next month, the residents feeling that, though he founded Utah, he was too much a religious symbol and had no place in a government building.

I found the mayor's office and walked past his secretary. My father was at his desk with two city councilmen discussing something about monster homes and stopping their development in some area of Park City. He glanced to me and said, "We'll talk more later."

I waited until the men left and then stepped inside his office and sat down across from him.

"You wanted to see me?"

He leaned back in the chair and rubbed the bridge of his nose with his fingers. "Tell me you didn't kill that girl."

"I didn't kill that girl."

He looked at me, his eyes steely and gray. Since I could remember, he had the ability to see through me when so few other people could. "Thomas, tell me you didn't kill that girl."

"I did not kill any girl."

He turned to a bottle of Vos water and took a sip. "When you were eight, your mother caught you cutting that neighbor girl... what was her name?"

"Cindy."

"That's right. Cindy. You cut her up so bad she needed plastic surgery. Your mother said you were sick. That you needed to be put away somewhere so you couldn't hurt anybody. I didn't see it. I just saw my boy. I had a streak of cruelty too and I thought I had rubbed off on you. I thought it would help you in the business world, in politics... I didn't recognize what you were."

"And what's that?" I said, my eyes locked to his, my voice even.

"You're an animal. And I'm through bailing you out. If you did anything to that girl you're on your own. I'm not helping you, not with the police, not with anybody."

"Someone dies and I'm the first person you look at? That seems hardly fair."

"You know when the last time we had a murder up here was? Then you move out and three months later we've got not one but two. And then an FBI agent."

"I moved out because you asked me to run the company."

"Yeah, and somehow you can actually keep it together long enough to do a decent job. How is that? How do you have that *thing* inside you and still function?" He chuckled. "You know what the VP said about you? Nate? He said you were one of the funniest, most charming people he's ever met. How is that, Thomas? Can you just put on that mask whenever you want?"

"Is there any real reason you called me here?"

"Yes, you're leaving."

"Where am I going?"

"I don't give a shit. You're just not staying here. Not anymore. And you're resigning from the company."

"I like it here."

"You like it here 'cause these small-town folk worship you. You drive up in a Ferrari and fly these girls out to the Caribbean and get blow jobs and you think that makes you a man? Well guess what, tough guy, this is mine. I earned this. You didn't do shit for this."

"If that's all," I said as calmly as possible, "I'd like to leave now."

He exhaled. "Sure, go. Go do whatever you want. But I want your resignation by Friday and you on the next plane outta here by Monday. If you're not on that plane, I'm calling the FBI and telling them to look into you."

"Bullshit. You can see through me but I can see through you, too. It would end your career if I was found to be the one that killed that girl, which I didn't. But you would be the father of *that murderer*. Forget mayor, you couldn't run a lemonade stand with the reputation you'd have. Helix's stock would plummet, too. You'd lose everything."

We sat and stared at each other a long while, neither of us saying anything.

I rose and unbuttoned the top button on my suit coat. "Always a pleasure, Father." Walking out of city hall, I stopped and looked to the mountains east of us and their snow-covered peaks, which looked like white foam pouring down over them and rolling to the bottom. I wasn't going anywhere. I liked it here. I liked running the company. I wasn't scared of my father or anyone else. The only things I cared about were amusement and curiosity, and so few things amused me or piqued my curiosity that when I found one, I had to use it for all it was worth. This town, and the degenerate fools that wasted their lives away in it, amused me.

At some point, my father would have to be dealt with. But not today. Today, I was in a good mood. Because I had decided on my next adventure.

JON STANTON

It was Thursday evening when I decided to call Emma. I hoped she had cooled down and was ready to discuss things with me, but somehow I knew she wouldn't be. She would be distant and cold. On an unconscious level, she knew the best way to hurt me was not to grow angry or break things or insult me, but to quietly withdraw her love. And she was a master at it.

She didn't answer and I left a message, something ridiculous about the altitude causing me to get dumber, and then I thought that I should take a little break.

I took out the scriptures app on my phone. I felt like reading the New Testament and I turned to Luke and began reading at a random location. The scriptures were familiar to me and comforting in a strange place.

I remember when I was baptized into the Mormon Church. Christians told me it was a cult and not to do it. Non-Christians told me you become a slave to any religion you joined. But I never saw it that way. Maslow's hierarchy of needs, an extensive study conducted on the needs of human beings, placed a sense of belonging as one of the most fundamental of all needs. Even above food and sex. Religion gave that sense of belonging. That was something atheists never understood when they questioned how an intelligent person could believe in talking bushes and an ark filled with two of every animal. In the end, it didn't matter whether it was true or not. The effect was nearly the same.

I was anxious and jittery so I could only read a few passages. Some condominiums not far from where I was had a pool. I'd seen them as we'd driven past the day before. I dressed in shorts and a t-shirt with sandals and walked the block and a half down there. The gate was open and at least thirty people were at the pool, most of them sitting on the deck.

I put my keys and phone and shirt on a deck chair and walked to the edge of the pool. I slipped my legs in and then my waist and torso. Quickly dunking my head under, I came up and spit out the water that was cascading down my lips into my mouth. The air was warm and there wasn't a breeze. I breast-stroked out to the other side, turned around with my back to the wall, and then put my arms against the edge and held myself afloat with my legs in front of me, letting the sun warm my face.

Right behind my eyelids images were flying past. I couldn't stop them and I couldn't slow them down. I saw a dark forest with twisted, black trees, their leaves dead. A woman was screaming as she ran in the darkness, the branches and rocks and shrubs scraping her legs and arms and face. Her breathing was heavy and strenuous and her legs hurt. She didn't know how long she could keep running. She had never been an athlete and had never needed to work out to maintain her slim figure. Exertion was unfamiliar.

And behind her was Death.

It moved on two legs but wasn't human. Her screams only excited him and her cries may as well have been given to the rocks or the trees. Death was just as indifferent.

The running was growing more difficult though adrenaline burned in her veins. He had adrenaline too, and he had prepared for this. He knew this moment would arrive. For her, this was lightning striking.

I saw her begin to slow and looked for satisfaction in Death but there was none. He doesn't care. This was all inevitable for him. Everything she had done in her life, all of her actions, led up to this. She didn't have a choice. And somehow, I knew Death didn't either.

He sliced her brutally on the first strike. A warning and a tactic to induce shock. Great white sharks used the same tactic on seals. They don't kill on the first blow but simply attack once, so viciously, that the seal loses their will to live and freezes from the inducement of shock.

He rips off her clothing, letting her know she can only wear what he tells her she can wear. He spends more time than necessary on the panties and makes sure she sees that he's cutting them off. He pulls down his own pants and tries to enter her, but can't. Something's wrong. Something he didn't plan for. Something he couldn't plan for.

The scene is too chaotic. Somewhere, deep in the recesses of his mind, he thought she would, on some level, succumb and become a slave, if only for a few moments.

But she cried uncontrollably and the blood caked her skin in the night. Black blood that was difficult to separate visually from the ground and it appeared like the earth was swallowing her.

He gets up and rips a tree branch off and returns to her. He'll be damned if she doesn't feel this. She will feel—

"Excuse me."

My eyes dart open and my heart is racing. I feel the water against my skin and blink several times as if I'd just woken up. A young boy is there next to me and he's holding on to the side because he can't swim and he doesn't trust the two inflatable orange tubes wrapped tightly around his biceps. I move away from the wall and he slides past me.

THOMAS FISCHER

Fur n' Things was the nearest pet store. I was in a strip mall that was called an outlet mall so they could charge whatever they wanted and people still thought they were getting a deal. As I pulled up I saw several older mothers dressed like teenagers, showing legs and cleavage, attempting to feel relevant. To feel desired. And if you showed them even a little desire, they would do whatever you wanted.

No one else was in the store and the girl behind the counter smiled at me and I smiled back. I walked among the cats and tapped on the glass of a little white one, who stuck his nose out. I rubbed it and it was wet and grainy.

I passed the cats and went to the dogs. Several puppies were out, as were about a dozen adult dogs.

"Can I help you?" said the girl, from behind me.

"Yes, I'll take these three puppies and then those two full-grown ones, and that cat, please."

"Um, you wanna adopt five dogs and a cat?"

"I have a ranch and I need some guard dogs. They'll have plenty of space." I walked back to the counter and took out my credit card and laid it down. "All six please, and I'll take six crates as well."

I drove up to Snake Creek in the Escalade and stopped in a thicket of woods. I took out the crates and set them in front of the car at the lip of the forest. Bending down, I let the cat out. He instantly darted away, sensing his freedom.

Then, I opened the crates to the dogs.

They barked like they'd been possessed and chased after the

cat. I sat on the hood of my Escalade and smoked a cigar and watched.

They all disappeared into the trees. A while after, the dogs wandered back. No blood. The damn cat had gotten away. Well, it deserved its freedom then.

I took out my Barnett Ghost 400, the best crossbow I'd been able to find. It used a noise dampening technology I wasn't totally familiar with but had tested several times and found that the arrow hardly made a whisper.

I began firing into a nearby tree. Over and over. The arrows crowding together in the bark. When I emptied the bag of arrows, I pulled them out of the tree and shot them again.

When I grew bored, I loaded the dogs back into their crates and headed back to the pet store to drop them off in front. They weren't worth killing. They wouldn't know what was happening to them.

For that, you needed a different kind of prey.

JON STANTON

Melissa wanted to have dinner that night and I said that would be fine. She picked me up at the motel and took me to a restaurant in a little town called Midway. It was founded by Swiss immigrants and had Swiss flags up on every block.

The restaurant, called Tarahumara, was near a hot springs and she suggested we go swimming there after and I said that I would watch.

It was a home-cooked-meal type place with wooden chairs and tables with red and white tablecloths. The waitress was dressed in jeans and a sequin shirt. Melissa ordered enchiladas and I had a pork burrito.

"So what made you want to quit being a cop?" she said. This was a loaded question as I had no doubt she had already looked me up and had seen some of the cases I'd handled.

One in particular haunted me: Michael R. Harlow. The former chief of police of the San Diego P.D.

I had to testify against him and it had brought down his entire administration. He was serving what would effectively be a life sentence in a federal penitentiary in Lompoc, California.

"You already know."

She grinned. "Yeah, I do. I wanted to hear it from you."

"It's not something I talk about."

"Having to testify against other cops couldn't have been easy."

"They were killing people that got in their way. They were worse than the people we chased because they were sanctioned by government to use force."

"Still couldn't have been an easy decision."

"No, it wasn't. On top of everything else, Mike was my friend."

The food came out quickly and we ate for a while and didn't speak.

"Do you ever regret becoming a cop?" she finally said.

"I wouldn't have met my fiancé if I hadn't. So no, I don't regret it for that. But if I had to do it over again, I might just have gone to medical school like my father was pushing me to. He was a psychiatrist and thought that that's what I'd be devoting my life to."

"You kind of did. You have a doctorate in psych."

"He thought psychologists were charlatans. He said that there's such an intense desire to stand out from the crowd that they'll publish any theory, no matter how ridiculous or harmful to the mentally ill. He also thought the people that went into psychology typically had deep emotional scars they were trying to deal with."

"Is that what it was for you?"

"Maybe." I smiled. "Or maybe I knew it was the one degree that would drive him the most crazy if I obtained it."

She laughed. "Sounds like me. My dad, when he was young, belonged to like an anti-government militia. He grew out of it but he was always a conspiracy theorist. He thought that 9-11 was perpetrated by the Bush administration, things like that. I think he almost had a heart attack when I told him I was going to be an FBI agent."

"What did your mother think?"

"She wasn't around. She left us when I was six."

"Do you ever think of finding her?"

"No. She's a stranger to me. I don't see what purpose it would serve."

"In my limited experience, I've seen it is as a release of anger in the child. They can't heal when they hold on to so much anger that they repress their natural curiosity for their birth parents."

She shrugged. "I think she's some junkie in Portland or somewhere. I don't know how much anger it would release to see her like that." She glanced up at me, holding my gaze a moment before going back to her food.

"You know, David told me something about you once."

"What was that?"

"We were talking about you after that big arsonist case you cracked open. About how the blogosphere was blowing up with rumors that you're psychic."

"David didn't believe in anything supernatural, so I'm guessing he put a stop to that right away."

"He did. And I asked him how it was that you had cleared so many cases. Ones that no one else thought could be cleared."

"And what did he say?"

"He said, 'Takes one to know one.'"

I was silent a moment and took a sip of water. "You think I'm a sociopath, Agent Harding?"

"I didn't say I said it, I said David said it. He said he thought you were a high functioning, extremely socialized sociopath that had put your disorder to good use. It sounds bad, but I think it gave him hope that we have a choice in the things we do and we don't have to choose to be evil pricks."

"Sometimes psychiatry creates disorders that aren't there. The DSM commission, the commission that determines what are actually classified as mental disorders and what are not, votes and argues. It's at the whim of personal prejudices. That's not science. Look at childhood bipolar disorder. Every reputable study done outside the United States has found that it does not, cannot, exist in young children. We're the only country that recognizes it and prescribes medication to three year olds for it."

"Why?"

"Because the pharmaceutical companies pushed for it. They don't even need to push that hard. A few grants here and there, some stipends, a few executive positions, and they have whatever they want from the psychiatric community. They tell us something's wrong with us and then offer the cure. That's exactly what snake-oil salesmen did a hundred years ago, though they didn't couch their deception as pure science."

"You and my dad should hang out."

I grinned. "Just because you're paranoid doesn't mean they're not after you."

The waitress came over and we ordered dessert and I asked for a refill of Diet Coke. My head was throbbing and sending waves of pain down my neck and shoulders. I took out a small bottle of Advil from my pocket and popped two of them and then drank down half the drink.

"This guy we're after," she said, "you think he's going to kill again, right?"

"Yes."

"How do you know?"

"This was his first time. He got a taste for it. After the first kill, when they see how easy it was and that the earth doesn't open up and swallow them whole, they don't think about anything else. It's like they've discovered a new toy. He's thinking about all the things he did wrong, everything he could've done better. He'll improve next time."

"When's next time?"

"At the beginning of their cycles they can wait long periods without having to kill. Later on, he won't be able to go more than a few weeks without it."

"What do you mean cycles?"

"Most serial murderers kill in cycles. I think they have a pattern they repeat, certain spacings in time between victims that ends after a certain number, and there's a long dormant period before they take it up again."

"How long do you think before he does it again?"

I shrugged. "I don't know. Right now, it's probably all he can think about."

3

On Friday morning, I woke as the sunlight hit my face. I'd gotten maybe three hours of sleep. At around one in the morning, I woke and couldn't go back down so I'd gone for a walk.

The streets had been wet from a light rain that I hadn't noticed. They shimmered and appeared like the lip of some black hole that I could just fall into at any moment and be lost forever.

Small towns at one in the morning always looked the same to me. An eeriness that couldn't be explained or described the next day always descended over them. Like a funeral on a stormy day. It gave you a dark, thick feeling in your gut.

I walked out of town and was on the road alone in the forest. The animals were quiet, sheltering themselves from the drizzle that was still falling out of a dark sky. No cars were on the road this late and the farther I went from town, the more alone I felt. Like I'd been dropped off in the wilderness.

I kept going until I hit a patch of road that was a steep incline. I was sweating and my legs began to burn from the acid build-up and I turned and headed back. In the darkness, with the ground reflecting any small glimmer of light, it didn't even appear like the same place I had just walked through.

Now, at six A.M., I wished I had taken something to help me sleep. My muscles felt weak and my mind was a blurry smear of thoughts. I took a cold shower and dressed and got into the rental car before driving to Café Lemon.

Parking near the front, I went inside and found a table near the window in the back. I ordered a muffin and Diet Coke and sat quietly, watching customers come and go, ordering large coffees with thick cream and lattes and steamers and copious amounts of pastries.

One of the waitresses was attractive, more so than you would expect to find someplace like this. I noticed that everyone who worked there was attractive, including the men. A cheap tactic by management to create a better experience, but one that, at least on men, typically worked.

The waitress was serving a table of men in biking gear and she bent over to retrieve a menu and all of them looked down her shirt.

I saw Tiffany here in my mind. Saw her bent over the same table and *him* staring at her. He lusted after her but the thought of having her permission disgusted him. There was no fun in that.

He sat here and watched as she helped other customers and gave them her beautiful smile. A smile he pretended was just his. She would do something when she thought nobody else was watching, maybe just biting her nails, and he thought to himself that that would be their secret. No one else needed to know about it.

He would sit here for long periods, sometimes her entire shift, but never say a word to her. He wanted to remain unnoticed. He would watch as her boyfriend would come pick her up and they would kiss outside and it would revolt him. Those were his lips. That was his kiss.

When he had her in the woods on her back, her organs cascading out of her slowly like melting ice, he tried to kiss her like that. But it wasn't the same. Her lips were pursed and crinkled and there was no affection, though he told himself there was—she loved him and he loved her and he would make her a part of him forever.

He took up her hand and bit off one of her fingers. He tried to eat it there but couldn't so he cut it off to not leave bite-marks. He placed it in his pocket instead and would take it with him. He took his knife and cut off a few more but the thumb wouldn't come off. So he... he went to the car. Her filthy little boyfriend was a landscaper. He had tools.

He took gardening shears out and went back to Tiffany who he'd tied to a tree. She screamed even more when she saw the shears. No one was out there and she was screaming to trees. He leaned his head back and screamed too, to show her it was pointless. Terror gripped her then and she quietly sobbed as he bent down and put her thumb into the shears... but stopped.

But stopped.

What stopped him?

This was his moment. His and hers. He wanted this for themselves. The only thing that would break the magic was... if someone else was there.

I glanced up at a man in a black pin-stripe suit who was standing in line. He turned away. I jumped up and headed out the door, my cell phone to my ear.

"This is Melissa," she answered.

"Have someone pull the financial records for Dale Christensen. You're going to see a large cash deposit in his checking or savings account the day after Tiffany was killed. Text me and tell me how much it was for."

"How do you—"

"Heading to the jail now to see him. Can you text it to me?"

A long pause before she said, "Gimme an hour."

THOMAS FISCHER

Heading into work, I felt like throwing up. I was agitated and thought I would smash in the face of anyone who looked at me funny. I masturbated in the car on the freeway but it didn't help. The emotions felt like a combination of someone really pissing me off and receiving terrible news at the same time. I was being pulled apart, and at one point I thought about running my car off the road and into a reservoir of dark blue water.

I stormed into work. Karen was at the front desk and smiled at me.

"Morning," she said.

"Why are you wearing pants?"

"What?"

"You look like shit. Wear a fucking skirt sometimes."

I walked past her as I went to my office and shut the door. I closed the blinds on the windows and lay down on the couch, staring at the ceiling. Outside, I could hear the hum of car engines and the occasional ding of the stupid trolley they had going up and down the street. From the office, all I heard were phones ringing and people talking. It was annoying me enough that I thought about opening the door and shouting at them to shut the fuck up.

Taking several deep breaths, I decided it was better if I just disappeared for the day. I left my office and stood in the hall. Then I walked into the first office I saw. It was owned by a pudgy man with glasses I knew as Hank or Henry. An analyst. A position that every Ivy League graduate would sell their own mothers for.

"Hank, how are ya?" I said, sitting down.

"It's actually Harold, Mr. Fischer."

"I prefer Hank," I said with a smile. "Listen, there's no easy way to say this so I'm just going to come right out with it. We don't feel you're contributing to our team in the manner we expect at this point in your career. We're letting you go."

All color left his face and I had to suppress a grin.

"You're firing me?" he gasped.

"Yes."

Tears came to his eyes. This was too funny. He leaned back in his chair and his belly thrust out of his shirt and I could see that one of the buttons was undone.

"I just got promoted like two months ago."

"An oversight that I'm fixing now. You're just not good at your job, Hank. And, between me and you, some of the girls have complained about your... well, your hygiene habits."

"Like what?"

"They said you smell and you're typically not pleasant to look at."

"What? Who said that? I don't smell."

I rose. "Get your things and get out, I don't want to have to call security. And Hank, if it makes you feel any better, you've put a smile on my face."

Walking out of the office I saw Karen sobbing in the break room. I thought about stopping and saying something, but didn't. I wanted to be out with someone else. With *her*.

I only knew her first name was Amanda and she was waitressing while she worked her way through school at Brigham Young University. Her major was education and she wanted to be a teacher for disabled children, or some other idiotic crusade.

I went across the street to Café Lemon and stepped inside and saw her across the restaurant. She was helping four douches in biking clothes, one of them still wearing his helmet like a moron. I felt like taking a hammer and bashing through it and showing him his brains. Picturing it made me laugh out loud. The elderly woman standing next to me was glaring and she turned away and put some distance between us.

The four douches looked down her shirt when she bent over the table. As she left they began talking about it. I stormed over there.

"Hi," I said. They didn't respond.

"Do we know you?" one of them said.

"No, but if you look at her tits that way again, I'm going to rip out your eyeballs and skull-fuck you."

"What? Fuck you, buddy."

I walked away. No use arguing in here. I glanced out the window and saw their bikes on the rack outside. I would just grab some coffee and go wait in my car. When they took off down the street, I'd follow them until we got to a secluded area and just take them out with my car. I was driving the Maserati today; it would get damaged but it would be worth it.

"Hi Tom," she said.

"Hey. You look nice for this early in the morning."

"Oh, thanks. You're so sweet."

"So any big plans for the weekend?"

"Just hanging out with my boyfriend and watching movies."

Boyfriend. I hadn't seen him. I didn't let my face show anything other than a smile. "Sounds like fun. You guys hanging out at his house?"

"No, I'm housesitting for my friend Michelle this weekend. They got that big cabin up there by Wolf Mountain."

"The one with the tennis courts?"

"Yeah, isn't it awesome?"

I smiled wider. "It is."

"So what can I get you?"

"Huh?"

"To drink. The usual? Non-fat latte with sugar substitute and an apple?"

"You know me well."

She grinned as she rang it up. "I usually have a chocolate chip muffin and coffee. You have such good self-control."

I glanced out the window. "If you knew me better you wouldn't say that."

As she made my latte I scanned the restaurant and was about to turn back when I saw something that made my heart drop into my stomach. My knees felt weak, and I thought how odd it was that it was an actual thing and not something made up in the movies.

Jon Stanton was sitting far back by the windows. He was staring off into space. Looking right at me but not seeing me. I'd seen that stare. It's called the predator stare. I saw it in my father when he got back from Vietnam. I saw it when I looked in the mirror.

He found me.

The media likes to make heroes and villains where there are none and I thought that's what he was; some cop who got lucky a few times and would come out here, strut around, and then leave and never return.

But he'd been here three days and he found me.

He wasn't a normal human being.

I turned back around quickly and stared at the counter. I wanted to run out of the restaurant and get into my car and drive to the airport. To never come back here. I couldn't imagine worse punishments than rotting in a cell, or having poison injected into my veins as the so-called victims' families watched my life sputter away. I was beyond them, beyond their understanding of what human beings could be. And I would be brought lower than a dog.

Stanton suddenly jumped up and ran out of the restaurant without a second look at me. I watched as he ran to a car in the parking lot.

"That'll be five-twelve, Tom."

As Stanton pulled away, I ran out, Amanda saying something behind me.

You should buy Jon Stanton dinner, Amanda, I thought. *Because he just saved your life.*

JON STANTON

I sped to the jail without realizing that I could've been pulled over. My phone buzzed as I jumped out of the car and ran in. It was a text with a single figure: $75,000.

The clerk behind the counter eyed me up and down and said, "Visiting hours are over."

"I need to see Dale Christensen."

"Come back tomorrow."

I glanced to her nametag. "Jill, that girl that was killed. Tiffany Ochoa. Did you know her?"

She was silent a moment. "No."

"But I bet you knew someone like her. I'll bet you have a daughter or a niece that was her. She was tortured to death, Jill. And Dale Christensen knows who did it. Please let me speak with him."

She hesitated, making a sucking sound through her teeth and glancing to the guard in front of the sliding metal doors leading to the cells.

"You got twenty."

"Thank you."

I ran past the guard, who didn't search me, and went to the room I'd met Dale in before. It took them a while to bring him here and I couldn't sit still. I paced the room. I stopped suddenly when something entered my thoughts: I was enjoying this. Maybe enjoying wasn't the correct word, but maybe it was.

Though Hawaii had been relaxing and pleasurable, I hadn't felt in the moment. It was as if I were standing outside of myself and watching the actions I was going through.

But right now, I felt in the moment. I felt my mind and body in sync with each other. I felt… at peace.

The door on the other side of the glass opened and Dale Christensen sat down in front of me. I waited until the guard left before speaking.

"Seventy-five thousand. I know it seems like a lot but I bet you would blow through it in less than six months."

"I don't know what you're talkin' about."

"Who is it?"

"I don't know nothin'."

"You didn't wake up in the morning. You woke up at night. You walked right on him when he had Tiffany tied to that tree. That's why he had to hurry, why he rushed. But I don't get why he didn't kill you. Why not just put an arrow through your heart?"

He swallowed and didn't say anything.

"This isn't you, Dale. You got issues but you're not a bad person. You don't protect murderers. Tell me who he is. Let me stop him from doing this again."

He ran his hand through his hair and exhaled. "I didn't... I—"

"You were in the moment and you weren't thinking."

"It wasn't that, man. I saw what he was doin' to her and he saw me. I took off. He chased me but I lost him in these woods, man. I know these woods. I live in a cabin in these woods."

"And you called him the next day and got paid."

"Yeah, man. Yeah, I got paid."

"How'd you know who he was?"

"Everybody knows who he is. This is a small community up here, man."

"Tell me who, Dale."

"I want immunity, man. I don't want no accessory charges. I don't need that shit."

"Tell me who he is, and I'll do better. It'll stay between us and you keep that money."

"I got your word?"

"You got my word."

He nodded. "All right, man. His name's Thomas Fischer. He's the mayor's boy."

I ran out of the jail and dialed Melissa's phone as I stepped outside. It went straight to voicemail.

"Thomas Fischer, Melissa. His name's Thomas Fischer and he's the CEO of Helix Financial. The mayor's son. Get some people down there now. I'm calling the Sheriff's Office. Call me back."

As I went to the driver's side door and unlocked it, I heard the door of the car next to me slide open: a van.

I glanced back just as the cloth went over my mouth.

2

I saw my boys on a beach. They were waving to me as the surf was foaming around them. They appeared younger and I could hear something, like a high-pitched squeal of metal. The sun was reflecting off the water and it was bright and causing spots in my vision. The boys began to fade away and I reached for them but they were gone...

The forest was speckled with light. I could see leaves and the rough bark of old trees. Birds were somewhere above, squeaking curiously at the invader in their home. The dirt underneath me was warm and soft and I didn't want to move.

My vision was blurry and I decided I wouldn't stand until it cleared. When it finally did, I rolled to the side first, feeling the pressure in my back and ribs, making sure they weren't broken. Then I sat up.

The sun was nearly above me, which told me it was sometime just before or after noon. I stood and noticed for the first time I was barefoot. I looked around for my shoes but didn't see them. I wasn't on any type of path. It was as if I had been thrown from a plane in the middle of the woods.

I was quiet and listened for the sound of any traffic, but there was nothing other than birds. In a different context, they would have sounded beautiful, but their mournful chirps and hoots now seemed ominous. I began walking forward.

The trees were thick and several times I couldn't get through and had to find a way around. I came to a small clearing and could see nothing around me but hills and trees and mountains. A small hill was not too far from here and I walked to it and began to climb. From up high, I figured I could see farther out and hopefully see a road.

I didn't think much about who had grabbed me or what had

happened. Instinctively I knew. And I didn't think twice about it. It was, from his standpoint, the correct move only if he were to kill me and then flee the country. Otherwise, he'd get caught. I had informed Melissa and the FBI should already be at his door.

The hill became steep up top and large patches were nothing but jagged rock. My feet got cut twice and I had to finally sit down and let them rest a second before cautiously trying to climb up again. I had to rest and then move, rest and move. It took so long to get to the top that I had nearly forgotten why I'd climbed up here in the first place.

I sat down and looked out over an expanse of treetops and grassy hills. No roads that I could see. I turned the other way and then another and another. There was nothing.

Waiting what I thought was a long time, I finally heard something. A buzzing. I looked up to see a small puddle jumper plane flying overhead. I stood and began frantically waving my arms and shouting but they couldn't see me. It was flying what I guessed was north. I headed down the hill, and in that direction.

3

Surprisingly, the forest could actually grow hot. Or maybe it was the humidity that stuck to my skin like watered-down glue. It was always there, and as the sweat rolled down my cheeks and the tip of my nose I hoped that I would come across a stream. You could survive for weeks without food but even two days without water could force your kidneys to shut down.

I had never been comfortable in forests. I'd grown up in Seattle and moved to San Diego when I was young. An affinity for the ocean was the only thing that I had with nature, particularly the Pacific. I couldn't leave its crystal waters for anything. I'd been to the East Coast and surfed at some of the major spots along the coast, but it wasn't the same. The waters had a greenish tint and were colder. I had to stay near the Pacific.

My feet were cut badly now and I was relieved when I heard a stream up ahead. The dirt turned to soft mud and it cooled and soothed my soles and toes. I stood in it for a while before sitting next to the churning water and putting my legs in up to my calves. I didn't know how sanitary it was to drink and I tried to look far up to see if I could observe its source, but the trees only allowed me to see maybe fifty feet.

I cupped my hand and thrust it in and came up. The water was clean and cold, so cold that I surmised it must have come from the mountains and wouldn't contain too many parasites. I drank and then lay back in the mud.

Leaves crunched behind me. It was soft, like the wind blowing them around, but it was there. I had nothing on me: not even my cell phone or keys. I slowly looked toward the noise behind me.

A figure was there.

I spun around to my stomach and jumped up. I ran at it as fast as I could, waiting for the arrow that would enter my heart and end my life in this damp, dirty forest. But it didn't come.

"Jon!"

Melissa slipped out of the trees. I stopped, my heart pounding so hard it was a thump in my ears. She was wearing a tattered business suit, her hair disheveled, her shoes missing. Though we had never once touched, she ran to me and put her arms around my neck and I put one arm around her, trying to catch my breath.

"Are you hurt?"

"No."

"How'd you get here?" I asked.

"I don't know. I was walking into my apartment and I heard something and then woke up here. I saw someone up on that hill. It must've been you."

"It was. Have you seen anybody else?"

"No."

I glanced around. "I saw a plane going north. I was heading that way."

"I saw it too."

I nodded. "I'm guessing you don't have your gun on you, do you?"

"No. My badge is gone too."

"That stream is probably safe to drink from. Grab a drink if you need one and let's go."

The day only seemed to grow hotter until the sun was finally setting and night began to descend. The forest got louder as darkness descended, as most of the animals were nocturnal. Or maybe they felt the fear that we were sharing and instead of thinking and talking all they could do was make noise.

We stopped underneath a large sycamore and I looked for something to make a fire with. I had never been in scouts and hated camping. I gathered some bark and twigs and then didn't know what to do next. So I sat against the tree with Melissa next to me and we watched the moon. Hanging over the mountains like a wound, it seemed to bleed black-gray clouds. The stars were sprinkled over the sky in uneven patches and I could see another plane, a commercial jet, flying by. Neither one of us bothered trying to get its attention. We were shadows in the dark.

"I hate the forest," she said. "When I found out I was coming to Utah, I cried."

"Not a country girl, huh?"

"City through and through. I grew up in Los Angeles and then moved to San Francisco. I didn't even see a forest until I came here."

"You're a lot safer here than in a big city. The chance of a snake or mountain lion attack is slim, but the chance of getting mugged or shot or hit by a drunk driver is much higher."

She was silent a moment. "What are we doing here, Jon? Why does he want us here?"

"I don't know," I said. But that was a lie. I knew exactly what we were doing here: we were prey.

We sat under that tree long enough to recover and we talked the entire time. Mostly just to have something to do, something to take our minds off of what was coming, the inevitable sound of someone trying to sneak up behind us and the quiet buzz of an arrow as it raced toward us.

"You ever miss it? The streets? Helping to make a difference?" she said.

"I don't know if I ever made a difference."

"I've seen your file, you made a difference. Your partner, the one that killed those two girls and escaped, what was his name?"

I found I had to spit it out, forcing the words. "Eli Sherman."

"Yeah. He had a badge and gun. How many more girls could he have killed if you didn't stop him?"

"I stopped him by accident. I looked in his closet one night when I was sleeping there 'cause my wife and I got into a fight. He had a little box with photos and panties, mementos. When I turned around he was standing there, looking at me. Without a single word we both knew everything about each other. He knew I would kill him, and I knew he would kill me." I looked to her and she was watching me. "There's a fierce storm coming. It's made up of a million little evils and it's going to swallow us whole. Before we know it, we'll be standing in carnage and wondering what happened. And the people that are supposed to lead us are the biggest perpetrators. You have to become a certain type of cop if you want to stop that storm. I know one, his name's Alma Parr. I'm not like him. I can't stop it."

"But you tried. That's all you can do."

"One of the last cases I remember in Homicide was an elderly disabled woman who was beaten to death. Her purse was stolen and we thought it was a mugging gone wrong. But when we traced a credit card purchase online, we found three kids. Twelve year olds. They beat her to death with their baseball bats they used at practice in school.

"Evil has a purpose. Whether it's power, or revenge, or pleasure. This didn't bring them pleasure. None of them thought about the purse until after the murder. There was no agenda. It was just an act done because they could do it." I stretched my legs out in front of me and leaned my head back against the tree. The bark was rough and uncomfortable. "I don't understand this new phenomenon. They have no discernible motivations, nothing that drives them. Not even an aversion to boredom. It's not evil in the traditional sense, it's something else. A black nothing. Like they're just irrational, unthinking clumps of meat drifting through the world. You have to be a very specific person to understand that and to choose to fight it. I can't anymore. I don't understand it. I'm just as lost as anyone else."

She sat silently and watched the sky with me a while and then she said, "You found this guy in three days, Jon. Without a single witness stepping forward and with one of the worst police investigations I've seen. Three days. I think saying you don't understand it is you trying to convince yourself of something, but I don't know what."

Suddenly there was a change in the air. A slight twist in the air pressure, almost imperceptible.

It wasn't until the arrowhead had scraped my scalp and embedded itself into the tree that I realized what it was. I fell to the side, a burning streak across my skull. Melissa didn't scream. She was instantly on her feet and dragging me around the tree as another arrow exploded. Bark flew into my eyes and stung my neck.

"Get up," she shouted, "get up!"

I stood but was dizzy and confused. Warm blood flowed down from my scalp and over my cheeks and down my neck. Melissa had my hand and was pulling me as I heard a puff of air and an arrow flew past us and was lost in the darkness of the forest.

Melissa cut through a thick patch of trees. Even if he fired several arrows at once, he couldn't hit us here. We were surrounded by too many things that would absorb the impact.

The more we ran, the more my senses were returning to me. I'd taken a blow to the head and I didn't know how bad the injury was. I could only feel the bleeding that was beginning to slow, and the pain in my feet as we ran over rocks and dirt and branches.

We ran until our legs hurt and neither of us could breathe. The darkness seemed to close around us and the trees caved in. The branches were reaching for us in the night and we couldn't see them as they pulled at our skin and clothes. I stumbled once over a log and fell flat on my face and Melissa helped me up.

She nearly ran into a tree but I could see it coming and pulled her out of the way. A look of surprise came over her face but she didn't say anything and continued along what seemed like a short path.

No more arrows and I began to pull back.

"We can rest here," I said.

"No we can't. Keep moving."

"I don't see him."

"You have a head wound, Jon. You're not thinking clearly."

"I need to rest, Mel. Please."

Mel was what I had called my ex-wife. I stopped and she stopped too.

"Please, I need to rest."

She helped me down as I sat in dirt and leaves. She checked my wound. Ripping off part of her shirt, she used it as a makeshift bandage and tied it as tightly as she could.

"I can't see how bad it is in the dark," she said.

"It's bad. I can't feel my toes."

"That's 'cause you're not wearing shoes. I have that too."

"Oh."

"Come on," she said, rising and taking my hand, "we can't stop."

4

I felt cold and we ran as long as we could, then we walked. The forest at night was cruel; every noise was a predator and every glimmer of light fearsome eyes. It felt as if everything was aimed at us, every tree a hiding place.

We ran so long that neither one of us had any clue where we ended up. The same forest scenery, the same moon, but nothing else felt the same. Even the air was heavier and harder to breathe.

Finally nearing exhaustion, Melissa stopped and collapsed close to a tree. She leaned against it and closed her eyes and tilted her head back and then forward.

"Can you hear that?" she said.

I listened. A crashing noise from up ahead. Something like static from a television... water crashing against rocks.

"A waterfall," I said, sucking for breath. "There might be a trail by it."

I helped her up and we walked.

Touching the wound on my head, I could tell much of the flesh was gone but I didn't feel a deep puncture. Then again, I may have been losing sensation. I tried to keep my eyes on Melissa as she was pushing through the shrubbery; the crashing of the waterfall getting louder.

The forest suddenly went quiet. I was wondering what had happened to the animals when I saw that I was looking up at the sky. Something had struck me in the back of the head and I'd fallen. A black figure was standing over me with something in his hands.

"Run!" I shouted.

Melissa ran. The figure lifted the thing in his arms. I twisted and kicked out its legs and it lost balance but didn't fall. It aimed at me and fired and I held up my arm. The arrow went through my forearm, the tip an inch from my face. Blood spattered into my eyes and I screamed from the pain that shot through me like fire.

I kicked at him as he came at me and I staggered to my feet. He swung and I ducked and struck with my good arm to his face. He kicked out into my chest and sent me sprawling back into some trees. I heard something then in the distance, almost like a muffled animal. I could see another dark figure farther out. It was Melissa and she was trying to draw his attention away.

"No!"

He lifted what I could see now was a crossbow and I ran at him. He turned it to me at the last second and the shot went off but it went wide and only grazed my shoulder. I was on top of him and he reached back and elbowed me so hard in the jaw I thought I would lose consciousness. I saw stars and felt myself going out, the world closing in to a pinpoint of black. I fought to keep conscious, jumped up, and ran.

I wasn't even sure which direction I was running but as the ringing in my ears subsided I saw Melissa in front of me, shadowy by the light of the moon. An arrow whizzed past my ear like a bee but I didn't stop or look back. We were at the lip of the waterfall now, and it was impossible in the darkness to see exactly how far down it was.

"We have to jump," I said.

"No, it's too far. We should—"

She closed her mouth and looked at me and I wondered if I had said something. She glanced down to her chest and I saw the tip of the arrow sticking out, bits of gore on the edges.

She collapsed and I held her. Sucking in breath like she was drowning, her muscles stiffened and then turned to jelly as life left her. I had her in my arms, oblivious to the fact that someone was running toward me in the dark. I put my hands over the wound to stop the bleeding, but it was too late. She was gone.

I stood up. The figure was loading another arrow and I saw his face in the moonlight. He was handsome and his wavy hair came down over his eyes. He looked up at me and our eyes caught like flint in the darkness, and he froze. We stood like this just a moment and time itself was still. I couldn't hear the rush of the water behind me or feel the pounding of my heart. I had made a decision and everything else came to a standstill.

I took a step back, and jumped.

THOMAS FISCHER

I couldn't believe that crazy bastard jumped. He was as nuts as the blogs and the newspaper articles said he was. I knew this land well and that was a fall of at least a hundred feet into water that only went down about nine feet, with jagged rocks sticking out. I stepped close to the ledge but the moonlight did not illuminate much and I lowered my weapon. He was probably dead, but I would have to make certain. *He saw my face. He knows my name, where I work, probably who my father is...* I had killed an FBI agent. They would scour the earth for me and find me in a hole like Saddam Hussein, broken and filthy.

I turned to the woman at my feet. Grabbing her by her ankles, I brought her to the ledge and kicked her over, watching the body tumble and disappear.

A trail was off to the left and I had to pull out my flashlight to find it. I began running down, careful to watch for branches, roots and rocks. Breaking my ankle out here, no one would find me for days. We were a three-hour drive from the nearest city and not many tourists knew about this place. Primarily bow hunters used it in the off-season. Park rangers and the locals had an agreement that what happened here would be between nature and the men that hunted. No one would be cited for any poaching. The rangers were mostly local boys themselves and their loyalties lay with the community, not the federal government.

I skipped over a small root and landed at an odd angle on a rock. My ankle twisted, I fell to my backside and slid about five feet before I came to a stop on some other rocks. I lay a moment staring at the sky, breathing hard, a soft euphoria coming over me. I felt like the world was spinning but I knew I hadn't hit my head. I just felt ghostly... like I'd found what I was put here to do.

I jumped up and continued down the trail until I got to the bottom. I scanned the surface of the water and then the edges around the pool. Would a dead body float? I had no idea. I assumed it would. But the currents pushed everything away from where the water was falling so he most likely would have washed up on the sides.

The pool itself was maybe the size of an Olympic swimming pool, not terribly large. I walked around the edge slowly, my flashlight scanning back and forth. I came to the other side and in the forgiving mud saw something. I bent down over it: they were footprints. And they led from the pool into the forest.

I raised my weapon and headed into the trees.

JON STANTON

The air rushed my face and I lost my breath. I saw only blackness below but I sensed that it was whirling toward me. I hit the water so hard it felt like concrete. My feet hit first and I bounced backward and when I submerged I went so far down I hit the bottom. I don't know how far it was but I had thought I might've broken my leg.

I crawled to the surface, gasping for air as I kicked to the side. I clawed up into the mud and lay there, trying to determine if I could walk. I raised myself up and put pressure on my leg and stood upright. I didn't think it was broken, or if it was the nerves had been damaged and I couldn't feel the pain.

I looked up to the waterfall. The moonlight was dim but I could see the black outline of someone standing at the lip. I didn't know if he could see me or not, but I guessed he couldn't because of the added darkness of the shade of trees and shadows.

Hobbling into the forest, I stopped and glanced back once. Melissa was gone. She had to be. I saw it, and yet I wasn't entirely sure. Had I jumped too soon? Had I just left her up there to be killed by him? I couldn't think about it now. I had to keep going. I didn't know why, because I had never been frightened of death before, but I had to keep going.

Once I got into the trees, I bent down quickly and said a prayer to the Lord for sparing my life, and asked that he grant peace to Melissa as she passed through the veil. And then I stood and ran.

About two hundred yards out, the pain in my forearm was so intense I had to stop and lean against a tree. The arrow had entered on the soft underbelly and was sticking out the top of my arm. Attempting to pull it out, I nearly fainted from the pain. The arrow had barbs and would've taken chunks of flesh with it. It would have to be left there.

I took off my shirt and wrapped it around the wound as tightly as I could to try and slow the bleeding. The pain was radiating up my arm and into my shoulders and neck. I had a migraine and every little sound was like drums going off in my head; every ray of moonlight, dim as it was, felt like a flashlight in my pupils. But I kept moving.

I was embraced in darkness. Entering a part of the forest where the canopy was so thick above me that I couldn't even see the sky, I felt like I was groping my way around rather than looking where I was going. But I'd been in darkness before.

When I was sixteen I'd fallen into a depression so deep I couldn't get out of bed. I'd had no desire to. The entire world, all of existence, had seemed futile and ridiculous. I wondered at the time how it was that people had the motivation to even go to work, knowing that their work was to put food in their stomachs to be used as energy so they could work. And then one day death would just come along and rob them of everything they thought was precious. It was all so pointless.

My father, one of the most respected psychiatrists in Washington State, tried everything to pull me out. He never said anything about it, but I know it cut him deep. With all his education and experience and theories and centuries worth of knowledge of the mind, he couldn't even convince his only son that life was worth living.

I was shy and mostly a loner at school so no friends came and saw me. Except for one girl. She knew me from a mathematics class and we'd spoken a few times but had never hung out. When she noticed I hadn't been to school in a few weeks, she came over.

She was Mormon, the first I'd ever met. She was polite and not pushy and asked me to come over to her house on a Monday for something called family home evening. It was some sort of ritual where a Mormon family, no matter how busy, would make time to spend that night with their loved ones.

I remember walking in and instantly feeling like those people cared about me. I had never met them before in my life. They had no conception of who I was or where I had come from, but they'd welcomed me with open arms. I hadn't actually known people like that existed.

We spent the evening playing games and having snacks and telling stories. Despite the intense inner pain I was feeling, the type that painted the world black, I had fun. As I was leaving, she gave me a copy of the Book of Mormon and a hug. Having nothing else to do during the days, I read it.

My father, seeing that nothing worked, transferred jobs to San Diego, hoping that the sunshine and fresh ocean air would snap me out of whatever was going on with me. I did heal, but the ocean was only part of it. I converted to the Mormon Church at eighteen and my father nearly disowned me.

He didn't care that it was the Mormons per se; he saw all religion as a scam perpetrated by the bourgeois on the working class. "The greatest hoax in the history of mankind," he called it. When I converted, our relationship changed. He didn't think you could be counted a man of the intellect if you believed in ghosts in the sky.

But science didn't mean the same to me as it did to him. In my darkest days I fell into the 18th and 19th century philosophers, and I knew from Kant that for every phenomena there were not one or two or even several, but an infinite number of possible explanations. This was the reason for the constant changing of science. Aristotle gave way to Copernicus who gave way to Newton who was upended by Einstein who was at odds with quantum mechanics.

And I knew that science would never reach an objective truth. Our species would go on infinitely changing our perspectives and models and theories, never stopping to ask if it had an end.

When I chose to abandon medical school for a PhD in psychology, my father had held out hope that I would attend afterward. When instead I applied to the police academy, it was another blow to our relationship and his view of my intellect. One that we never recovered from. He told me that power would corrupt anyone, no matter how nobly you applied it.

I thought of him now as I trekked through the dark with an arrow sticking out of my arm and my head bleeding into my eyes. The pain he would've felt that this is how my life would end. That, with the intellect he gave me, this was what I had chosen to do with it.

I stopped and glanced around. Everything was black and every direction looked the same. It didn't matter where I chose. So much blood was pouring out of me I couldn't run for much longer anyway, and even if I could, where would I go?

And worse, everyone I'd ever cared about had told me this is how I'd end up. My ex-wife Melissa, for a decade, tried to get me out of police work. She understood that you couldn't chase monsters without having them consume you, or becoming one yourself.

I couldn't extricate myself, even long enough for me to see she was slipping away from me. By the time I realized what was happening, she was gone.

Michael R. Harlow, my first boss as a police officer, also saw my background and asked what the hell I was doing as a police officer. I had no real answer for him other than vagaries about doing good and helping others. He'd looked at me a long time and said, "Leave, right now. This is going to be your last chance. Because if you stay and fall in love with it, you'll never leave. And you'll lose everything else in your life."

Even my partner, the only one I had truly bonded with, Eli Sherman, had told me that police work wasn't for me. That it would eat me up and he would one day have to visit me in an asylum.

Emma was only the latest. She had made a pact with me that if I left police work she would date me. I left and became a private investigator and nothing changed. I still chased madness through the streets. In order to marry me, she'd made me promise one thing: no more crime. I had to find something else to do.

I realized, only now, that I had broken that promise. I hadn't seen this as a case I was working. I had come because my friend died. But that was simple rationalizing. I had missed the chase, and since I had left it I hadn't felt complete. I wondered if she was already gone.

I sat down. There was no use running. Everything I'd done in my life, all of my actions, had led me to this point. I'd seen this point in my dreams as a child, that I would die alone in the dark. Whether now or fifty years from now, what was the difference?

My arm was causing intense pain and it hurt to sit. I lay back and stared at the canopy above me, moving with the wind like whirling phantoms.

THOMAS FISCHER

I moved cautiously away from the pool and into the forest. Once I was past the tree line, I felt alive. Something was awakened in me and I went from gently walking on my toes to keep the noise down to jogging through the thick shrubbery.

Hunting had been the one activity I truly enjoyed as a child. My father had taken me hunting several times but even he couldn't keep up with my voracious appetite for it. I was never interested in school or sports, video games or friends. Girls held a mild fascination for me, but other than sexual appeal, I found them uninteresting.

The forest was alive with sounds. Between the animals and the insects and the birds I could barely hear myself think. But I enjoyed it. I'd come up here years ago as a teenager on vacation from boarding school in Connecticut and stripped nude and hid behind the trees, pretending I was a werewolf on the prowl. I would look for things to hunt in the night and wished that someone would just happen by my path, but they never did.

Not until Tiffany Ochoa.

She was so beautiful when I saw her, so perfect. I knew she would be the one, the first one, the one I would remember the rest of my life. I wanted our night to be special but she had brought her boyfriend. She thought she was coming to a party, and when they stopped on the road where I'd wanted them, I put an arrow through his face first. I wanted her to see what he was—nothing but a sack of jelly encased in skin. She never did see that, I think, not even when she died.

Bushes rustled to my left. I stood frozen, the crossbow in my hands. I ducked low and aimed. Then some bushes farther out made the same noise. It was moving away from me.

I sprinted and fired but nothing happened. I loaded another one.

The branches whipped my face and I nearly broke my ankle on the soft forest floor but I didn't stop. I dashed forward so violently I noticed I was grunting and it made me laugh. I stopped and just kept my eyes forward as I closed in on him...

The raccoon hissed at me before disappearing into the brush. I was out of breath and glanced around. I had run so far off the trail I wasn't sure where it was anymore.

I lowered my weapon and lifted the flashlight, going slowly from tree to tree, backtracking where I had been.

JON STANTON

I saw my boys again. Mathew was a grown man now. He was working as a police officer in some suburb of New York and I saw that his jawline had grown to that of a man's; his once high-pitched voice flattened out.

He was working cases indifferently and I saw him pocket a load of drugs from the car. My eyes followed him as he was home now and sitting on his couch. He prepared the needle and cooked the heroin in a spoon with a lighter and sucked it up in the syringe before injecting the warm fluid into his arm. Instantly, his eyes dimmed and he began to nod and fell back on the couch and stared at the walls.

I saw Jon Junior. He was coming home from work and his wife was there and she was drunk again. He was upset and they were yelling at each other. Then without provocation he reached back and slapped her hard across the face.

The slap felt like it had hit me, and was so pronounced I woke up. I was lying on the forest floor. The moon had shifted and was somewhere near me and the light was coming down and speckling the trees with white spots.

I sat up. My boys... my boys. I had abandoned them, neglected them. I'd left them to the whims of their mother and her new husband without considering what it would do to them. I told myself it was for their own good, that she was a better mother than I was a father. But it wasn't true. The boys had bonded to me early. They would never recover from this. From the headlines they would read online about the ex-Homicide detective who had been found dead in a random forest, without ever having said goodbye to anyone.

My boys needed me as I had needed my father. He had never

been there and I had chosen a path in my life that I wasn't sure I would have chosen had he been there. Had I chosen this life just out of spite? Did I know that nothing would drive an aristocratic intellect more crazy than a son who worked a blue collar job? I hoped that wasn't it. But I couldn't be sure.

I pulled myself to my feet. I would live. Or at least try to.

Walking until my feet were so bloodied and achy that I had to sit down, I saw the canopy thinning out and could see more now in the light of the moon. The soles of my feet were black, as the blood made everything on the forest floor stick to them like glue. I tried to pick off some of the pebbles and twigs as best I could.

As I rose, I saw what looked like an indentation. I walked to it and looked down. It was a trap of some sort. Dug maybe five feet down. Or maybe it was a natural phenomenon? But I didn't think so. It looked like a pit meant to catch a bear or wolf or deer. It was manmade.

I glanced around at the tall trees and then to the pit again.

Working quickly, I began ripping down branches and laying them across the hole. It took four to cover it. Then I took dirt and leaves and spread them across the branches until it was difficult to tell it apart from the ground. I glanced back and then forward again. My head was spinning and the shirt wrapped around my arm had been completely soaked through. I was bleeding to death.

I walked around the hole and lay down on my side, and waited.

2

Looking out into the darkness, all I heard was my own breath, though the sounds of the forest were loud. They quieted a little farther out and I knew that meant something large was moving through that area.

My eyes were open from fear and anticipation and I tried to control my breathing. I could hear it clearly now, the soft sound of leaves crunching. Maybe twenty feet out and coming closer with each step. I was trying to tell if it was large enough to be him or if it was just some forest animal, but I had no frame of reference.

The soft crunching was near. Maybe ten feet behind me. I closed my eyes, convinced that I could hear better that way, and heard the footsteps stop a moment. They were deciding whether to keep moving forward.

They started again and I heard an unmistakable click: an arrow locking into place. Maybe five feet now. He wanted to see if I was dead or he had something to say to me. Some last jab before he took my life. Or he wanted to see me scream. He wanted the screams so badly that he was reckless.

A few more steps and then...

A surprised shriek and the tornado of branches breaking as he fell through into the hole. I twisted around in time to see his hand grab my leg for something to hold on to. The force pulled me down and I clawed at the ground with my fingers but they slipped through the soft dirt like air and I fell hard onto my back.

He was in front of me now and didn't have the crossbow. He ran up and, with a grunt, kicked my face and sent my head flying back. He tried again and I caught his foot and twisted it enough to cause pain and he pulled it away.

I got to my feet and saw him put his hands up in a boxing stance. He came at me with a jab that connected to my nose, and then jabbed again. He was too fast for me to see and he connected with at least five other blows before I kicked into his knee and slowed him down.

"How's the arm?" he said with a chuckle.

He flew at me and kicked into my groin and came up with an uppercut as I dipped down. It sent me back but he didn't stop. He hooked me so hard in the jaw I felt bits of teeth loosen in my mouth. Then he did it again and sent me sprawling onto my back. He was younger and faster.

My vision spinning, my arm feeling like it was about to be ripped away from my body, I saw the shadow stand over me. He seemed monstrously tall and he reached down from that height and struck me again in the face. Then he bent down.

"I have to say, if nothing else, you've entertained me quite a bit." He sat down in the dirt. "You want to know something? Something funny? You were expecting to find the devil, weren't you? Well, I'm not the devil. I had a normal childhood, I had parents that loved me, I was never deprived of anything. And still, the first time I wanted to kill someone I was four years old. It's just something that's part of me. How do you expect to stop that, if it's just a part of people?"

"I have something for you," I said, feeling bits of teeth in my mouth with my tongue. I spat them out.

"Oh, yeah? Some great insight, huh? Well, Detective, let me hear it. What do you have for me?"

I swung my arm with all the strength I had left. The arrow tip sticking out of my forearm latched into his eye and he screamed. As he instinctively jerked away the barbed tip tore out the eyeball and some of the stalk it was connected to.

He screamed so loud it was deafening. He fell to his back and rolled over in pain, his hands covering half his face like that would bring the eye back. I crawled over to him. He hit me in the face and I nearly blacked out. I fell on top of him and he was writhing so badly he didn't even notice.

He grabbed my throat with both hands. Anger was making him froth at the mouth and he was grinding his teeth loud enough to hear. I lifted my arm and swung down. He let go of my throat and caught my arm with one of his hands.

Putting all my weight into it, I pressed toward his throat, but he was much stronger. He was pushing me off. I lifted my other hand and thrust my fingers in his eye socket. I grabbed something slippery and soft and pulled as hard as I could until it ripped.

He screeched and let go of my arm and tried to get to his back. The arrow in my arm, the eyeball still attached, entered the side of his neck. I don't know how far it went because the pain was so intense I vomited. He swung back and bashed me in the head with a rock laying by him.

I was awake only long enough to look at the sky one more time before I blacked out.

EPILOGUE

Emma was on the beach in a lounge chair watching some surfers when she got the call. She had never come out to watch surfers before and wondered if she did it now because she missed him. It'd only been a few days, but she missed him and she hated herself for it.

The sun was reflecting off the cell phone in a way that she couldn't see the caller and she didn't care to. She knew who it was. She had known the moment Jon had flown to the mainland chasing ghosts of dead friends.

Reluctantly, she answered it.

"This is Emma."

"Ms. Lyon? This is Sheriff Wendy Cannon at the Heber Sheriff's Office. I have some bad news…"

The flight was a long one and she tried to sleep and then tried reading and finally two shots of vodka with orange juice calmed her enough that she slept the final hour.

It was a simple matter to rent a car and drive from the airport to the hospital, but it took her nearly two hours. The canyons were ominous in the fading daylight and the forest closed in around the little road like a hand closing around a stick.

The GPS led her directly to the hospital without issue and she parked in the ER parking, though he wasn't in the ER anymore. She took the elevator up to Intensive Care and a guard, a portly policeman with a button missing on his shirt, was reading a *Sports Illustrated* in front of the room.

"I'm his fiancé," she said.

The officer let her in with a quick check of identification and she pulled up a chair and sat next to the bed. He was on a ventilator and the low rhythmic rasp made her uncomfortable. The intubation tube running down his throat was clear but it stretched his skin in an odd way and made it look like plastic. In fact, his entire face looked surreal, like a mask that had been placed on a skull and then painted over.

She was there all night, even though the nurse came and offered to let her sleep in the room next door. She declined and stayed there. At one point, at around three in the morning, she couldn't sleep from bad dreams and so she took out her phone and opened the Kindle app and read *Les Misérables* out loud. It was his favorite book.

By six in the morning, she couldn't keep her eyes open any longer and she took up the nurse's offer to sleep in the next room. All the noise of a hospital was there, including the patients moaning about the pain they were in and the doctors and nurses talking about how annoying they were behind their backs. This was all taken in by her on an unconscious level, absorbing bits and pieces of a conversation here and there when she was woken by too much noise.

The rest of the days were not much better. The hospital food was atrocious and she would walk the streets of the town and try every diner and restaurant and dive bar there was. Anything but the hospital cafeteria.

Days ticked away and the doctors began telling her that the chances of a comatose patient awakening after forty-eight hours were slim. It was an exponential decline, one of the doctors said. Each day increased the odds that he wouldn't wake up the next day.

He had suffered a severe head trauma and skull fracture. The musculature of his left forearm had been torn away so violently they had to perform reconstructive surgery on the muscles and tendons connected to his ulna. He had lost so much blood they'd pumped it into him that first day and his body had drunk it like an endless pit.

But she didn't leave his side. She stayed there every day and read to him and fixed his hair and clipped his nails and helped the nurse with a sponge bath. She'd never believed in a God and found she didn't have a tongue for praying, but she knew how important it was to him. So she took out the Bible or the Book of Mormon and read passages to him at night in a quiet voice.

And one day, as she was reading in Matthew about Christ resisting Satan in the wilderness, he talked back.

Jon Stanton wrestled with a shadow. For a moment he was terrified that it wasn't real, that it was all in his mind and that chilling instant he had been dreading his entire life was here: when the mask of sanity slipped off and madness revealed itself.

The shadow caused pain and he remembered the taste of blood in his mouth and didn't know if it was his or not. He remembered darkness, like a long hallway with a mirror at the front, and he caught a glimpse of himself.

The hallway was dark on both sides and it filled him with dread. He was on a path, and it seemed like maybe it led somewhere, but he wasn't sure as he walked it. His stomach in knots, a general uneasiness came over him. The darkness encompassed everything and there were no lights but he knew he needed to keep walking.

He heard a voice behind him and stopped. He turned to it. Monotone, like it was reading something, sweet with a tinge of pain to it. It sounded vaguely familiar and he shouted for it but no words came out of his mouth. He ran toward it and came to a place where the tunnel ended and dim light was coming through. He looked back to the tunnel and didn't want to leave. It was pleasant.

He heard the voice again, and then a new one: it was his son.

Looking back one more time, he walked into the dim light and then remembered hazy outlines of people in front of him. A nurse, though he didn't know her name. His sons were sitting next to the bed, their mother out in the hallway speaking to the doctor as Emma sat in a chair and read to him, the boys listening intently but staring at the floor.

His voice, cracking and weak, quietly said, "And angels came and attended to him."

His son Matthew was the first to touch him. It hurt in a way touching had not hurt before and he felt nauseated. Emma sensed his pain and gently pulled Matthew away, but Jon Junior gave his father a hug. Emma reached down and held his hand, a weary, melancholy smile coming over her face.

Later that night, Stanton was alone with his ex Melissa as a physical therapist was stretching his limbs. Tendons shrink during inactivity and many coma patients would curl into the fetal position as their limbs shriveled around them.

"I want the boys," he said.

"Why?"

"It's very important to me, Mel. I can give them a good life. It doesn't have to be permanent, but I want them for a while. They'll have a lot of fun on the island."

She glanced out the window in the despondent way she always would when she had to do something she didn't really want to do. "We'll talk about it," she said. "You nearly got killed. I don't know if I can expose them to that. That... whatever it is that you have. It's not a gift, Jon. And everyone around you is exposed to death because of it. That's why I left. That's why she'll leave you, too."

The words stung and as Emma came back later after Melissa left, Stanton knew it was true.

They sat quietly a long time and Stanton listened to the hiss of the bed next to his adjusting behind a curtain. A man had been brought in that wasn't there before and he couldn't remember when that had occurred.

Finally he asked, "What happened to him?"

"Car accident I think."

"No, not him."

"Oh. He was dead on arrival due to blood loss," she said.

That was the extent of their conversation and all Stanton

could think to say to her. Both of them had a sense of what was coming but neither wanted to articulate it. It was an awareness that destiny had played its hand, that no matter how much they wanted to stay together and grow old together, it was impossible now.

"You should leave," he said.

"Leave the hospital?"

"No, Emma. You should leave."

"Don't be silly," she said, standing and adjusting his sheets.

"You won't leave now, or this year or maybe two years, but you'll leave. You've already made up your mind. You think it's inappropriate to leave now because I was injured, but you'll leave. Please just do it now. I can't stand to watch you slowly withdraw from me."

Tears filled her eyes and she continued adjusting his sheets though they didn't need it. When she was done, she held his hand and bent down and kissed him and then turned and walked out of the room.

As the physical therapy brought strength back to him, Stanton would spend his days walking the halls in a slow gait that reminded him of the old *Frankenstein* movies he watched as a kid. He met an elderly neurologist in the bed next to him. His name was Herb and he was recovering from a broken hip caused by an automobile accident. They spent time together every day watching the History Channel or Discovery Science.

Stanton was in his room as they watched an old science-fiction TV show on a cable station. He stared blankly at the screen and wasn't engaged at all, but he liked the flickering pictures. It was movement. Something about the movement comforted him and he didn't know what.

"I couldn't help but overhear the other day," Herb said. "I'm sorry."

"For what?"

"For her. It's one thing when they leave or you leave, but it's something else when you both just know it's over and it's nobody's fault. That happened to me and my wife. You know what that saint of a woman did? She stayed with me. She didn't love me, she knew it was over, and she stayed with me because she didn't want to hurt me. She would rather spend her life in a loveless marriage than hurt me. I wish I'd had the guts to do what you did. I think if I truly loved her and I wasn't a coward, that's what I would have done."

"I don't feel much like a hero right now."

"When heroes do something heroic I bet they don't either." He looked to Stanton. "If you really want her though, when you get out from this bed you'll go after her and try and make it work."

Stanton was in his room preparing to leave on one of his walks when he saw a man in a black suit and dark tie enter. Kyle Vidal looked like he stepped out of a television show and his skin was tan and smooth. He smiled as he shook Stanton's hand and sat down in the chair near the window where Emma had sat all those days.

"I came and checked up on you when I was out here for Melissa's funeral," he said. "It was odd seeing you that way."

"Wasn't much more pleasant from my end," he said, sitting down on the edge of the bed and using a cane for balance.

"How's the recovery?"

"It's good. They think I should be out of here in the next few days."

"You going back to Honolulu?"

"I am."

He glanced out the window. It was dawn and a frosty mist hung over the city and gave the trees a damp look that made him think of Virginia. "I'm sorry as hell this happened."

"You lost two agents, Kyle. They took the brunt of this."

He nodded. "David told me once you were the best detective he'd ever seen. He said he bugged you constantly about applying to the Bureau."

Stanton grinned. "He used to send me applications already filled out and waiting for a signature. He thought that's why I wasn't applying. Just out of laziness."

"Yeah, he was unique." Kyle was silent a moment and then dipped into his pocket and came out with an ID badge. "I've known two people like you in my time, Jon. One was a detective when I was with Miami Homicide. He could just put himself in the place of others, victims and perpetrators. He knew where to look for everything to clear a case. But he was never arrogant about it. He treated everyone, even serial murderers, with respect. But it drained him. Every single case drained him a little bit. And he decided he couldn't do it anymore so he retired, thinking that was the answer… and he drank himself to death one night on cheap whiskey.

"The other person applied to the Bureau from Phoenix Special Victims. Same thing. An amazing investigator, tenacious and smart. She threw herself into her work and kept getting promotion after promotion. She's the SAC of my office now. She's still helping, and she's still fighting the same fight, but her life's not at risk and she goes home to her family at five P.M. every night. She's earned that." Kyle threw the badge on the bed and Stanton could see the photo. It was himself with the blue FBI lettering stamped on top and the Department of Justice seal to the left. It said, SPECIAL AGENT JON STANTON and there were a series of letters and numbers underneath that.

"It's up to you," Kyle said, "which path you take. You can take that badge and come out and meet me at Quantico. Or you can go back and think you're retired. It's up to you." He rose and walked to the door and turned to him. "I'm glad you're feeling better. I really am."

Stanton watched him leave and lifted the badge. He stared at it a long time and then placed it back on the bed before going for his walk. He glanced out the window as he left and saw the sun poking through dark clouds far in the distance.

Printed in Great Britain
by Amazon